P9-DDU-221

0/Θ

SILVO

Temperly told himself he was a loner. But was he as much a loner as his old gunfighter friend Silvo, who now needed his help? Killers were on the loose, torturing and pillaging. Then there was the rich rancher whose son was a robber. The old man also had a beautiful daughter and, as Temperly well knew, Silvo was a devil with the ladies. Tansy with the big blue eyes waited for Temperly, but first a terrible job would bring gunfire, stampede and death.

Books by Vic J. Hanson
in the Linford Western Library:

KILLER ALONE

VIC J. HANSON

SILVO

Complete and Unabridged

LINFORD
Leicester

First published in Great Britain in 1994 by
Robert Hale Limited
London

First Linford Edition
published 1996
by arrangement with
Robert Hale Limited
London

British Library CIP Data

Hanson, Vic J.
Silvo.—Large print ed.—
Linford western library
1. English fiction — 20th century
I. Title II. Series
823.9'14 [F]

ISBN 0–7089–7881–9

Published by
F. A. Thorpe (Publishing) Ltd.
Anstey, Leicestershire

Set by Words & Graphics Ltd.
Anstey, Leicestershire
Printed and bound in Great Britain by
T. J. Press (Padstow) Ltd., Padstow, Cornwall

This book is printed on acid-free paper

Prologue

"LAST time I saw this much blood," said Silvo, "was in a slaughterhouse in Chicago. Went to visit a sick aunt there. Hated the place. Goddam mudhole. Ain't been since. That aunt died long since anyway."

"Didn't know you had any kin at all," said Dooley.

"Ain't now, I guess. Not properly. That aunt wrote to me. A scrawl. Claimed to be my mother's younger sister. Can't remember my mother an' whether she's alive or dead. Aunt didn't know. Was part Injun. The aunt I mean. Never knew my father, no more'n I did."

"I'm older'n you," said Dooley. "I've seen what Injuns can do. This looks sort of like Injun work. But there ain't any Injuns round here, is there?"

"Not so's you'd notice much." Silvo looked about him. "I've seen dead before an' I've seen blood. Dead is dead an' blood is blood. We'll have to look closer an' further if we want to make any sense of this lot."

"It doesn't make any sense at all," said the older man.

"Somebody did it all for somep'n," said Silvo.

He was young, but if looked at quickly or in certain ways he could have been thought of as old. Considerably older than his actual age anyway, and he wasn't himself quite sure what that was.

He was lean and dark and thin-featured. He had prematurely white hair worn pretty long and pale blue eyes which had a peculiar fixed look about them sometimes.

There were folks who thought Silvo was a pretty queer duck. Some of them were scared of him, and maybe with good reason. He was an accomplished gunfighter and a loner who went off at odd times and for odd periods, and he'd been seen in odd company in odd places.

None of this fazed Silvo at all. The folks he respected could be counted on four fingers of one of his lean brown hands. Dooley was his friend. He respected Dooley, though he'd never been able to figure out why. Outspoken, cantankerous, nosey old bastard!

He was following Dooley now, who was sniffing like a hound dog. Dooley was stooped and scrawny. He had very little hair but what he had wasn't as white as Silvo's. Dooley had been a redhead and his sparse locks now looked like dead weeds.

"This ain't been done long," he said. "The smell ain't too powerful yet."

"It's powerful enough for me," said Silvo and he drew his bandanna up over his mouth and nose.

It was early morning and the sun was now coming up, its pale rays filtering through the long, broken window which was the first thing the two men had noticed when they approached the place. There was no blood outside, no bodies, no sign of disturbance.

The sweet morning air came through the windows, but it couldn't dispel that other not so fragrant odour which had grown in the night and would get worse in these warm climes.

"Jolen fought hard," said Dooley: "That's why the blood's spread so."

"He's been hacked to pieces," said Silvo. "And the boy."

"He fought too. Only sixteen but a strong an' allus willin' lad."

"The woman!" said Silvo and, holding his bandanna to his mouth, he strode past his companion and walked through the open communicating door into the back room. This was a long one-storied log cabin with a sitting-room and an annexe kitchen at front and sleeping-quarters behind, the man and wife's, and, off at the side, a cubby behind a thick curtain for the boy.

Dooley followed the younger man, almost cannoned into him for, after his precipitate entrance, Silvo had come to a dead stop. He uttered a whispered blasphemy which was half between a prayer and a curse.

The woman was on the bed and she had been treated worse than the two males. She was tattered and mutilated flesh in a tumble of bloodied bedclothes. It would have been hard to determine what she had gone through, whether she had suffered greatly or whether she had been quickly dispatched and the devilries inflicted on her afterwards.

Dooley went round Silvo and over to the bed and he pulled up the bloodsoaked and tattered blankets to cover the body as best he could.

"Why?" said Silvo. "What for?"

Dooley shook his head slowly from side to side, unspeaking.

"We've got to find out," said Silvo, and he began to range the bedroom in a seemingly aimless way. There was a lot of blood but no sign of a struggle as there had been in the other room.

Still unspeaking, Dooley watched his young friend. He knew something about Silvo that he was sure nobody else in this territory had known. And he knew about that poor thing there on the bed, knew about her and Silvo.

Silvo wasn't looking at the bed any more and Dooley couldn't blame him. He thought Silvo was handling himself well.

Still and all, he had heard folks refer to the white-haired man, among other things, as a cold-hearted bastard. And a killer. Yes!

Hell, I don't know, he thought, and suddenly he felt immeasureably old.

He went through the motions, tailed Silvo, bent, peered. They found nothing, and they went back into the other room. Silvo called it, 'looking for clues', but again they found nothing that could be called such and they were glad to get out into the fresh air once more.

Their horses were waiting patiently. The Jolens had some stock in the small corral and that hadn't been touched it seemed. The terrible questions clustered, incongruous in the lively air of the bright morning; and there were no answers.

It was as if Dooley had mulled over his companion's queries, striving to make sense of them, of all of it, and had come back to his original conception. No sense, no sense at all.

"The Jolens didn't do anybody any harm," he said. "They didn't deserve this."

"Nobody could deserve this," said Silvo.

Dooley thought, what do you deserve, son? It was a fleeting thing, like a shadow, and didn't stay with him.

Silvo was moving again and Dooley followed him around the back of the building and to where they could see the lines of the town blossoming in the morning sunshine.

From the back the Jolen place looked the same as it always had as you approached it from town. Dooley and Silvo this morning had approached it from the other direction, coming in on it from the front, coming in from the older man's small horse-ranch which was a few miles further on.

All the ground both front and back was pretty churned up, or rock hard in some places, dependant on how the hot sun hit it. And the sun around here could be, at its zenith, pretty fierce. There were hoofmarks, but none of these looked particularly fresh. They told the searchers nothing.

"We'll have to go on an' get the law," said Dooley.

"Leave them like they are, you mean?" said Silvo.

"We-ell, we could wrap 'em in tarps or somep'n an' put 'em in the shade. But, apart from that, I think the law should look at the place pretty much the way we found it."

"I guess you're right. Though what ol' Oscar Brake 'ull make o' this is anybody's say so."

"It needs some kind of a detective at that, I guess," said Dooley.

8

"You're right," said Silvo.

They went back to the house and did what they meant to do. Then, as they rode, Silvo seemed sad, as, Dooley thought, he surely should be. But pensive sort of also, and unspeaking, almost as if he knew something that Dooley didn't, wondered, whether he could communicate this knowledge to his old friend or not.

After entering the cabin of death the two men had taken off their hats and put them on the window-sill. There was no blood there. They couldn't figure how the window had gotten broken so badly. Shards of glass lay on the bare boards beneath it. There had been little glass on the beaten dirt outside and no footprints either.

It appeared that, mainly anyway, the glass had been shattered from the outside by something pretty heavy. Or had shots been fired through it?

It would be difficult to ascertain whether the murdered folk had been shot before the terrible mutilations had been inflicted upon them.

Dooley, who had seen many things, had muttered about torture and sadism. He didn't know whether Silvo had heard him or not.

Now they had their hats back on and the morning breeze was in their faces and the sun was not yet very hot.

Dooley wore a battered Stetson with a hole in the crown. He'd won it from a sailor far from the sea in a poker-game.

Silvo wore what could be almost called a sombrero. A black one at that, for the lean, dark young man with the striking silver-white hair favoured dark things. The brim of his hat wasn't maybe quite as wide as that of an average Mexican sombrero, but Silvo had it pulled right down over his eyes now, and he wasn't saying a word.

A dark one with dark thoughts . . .

1

DAGGART was anybody's meat now and that was an undisputed fact. There was a price on his head. Dead or alive.

Cal Temperly was no bounty-hunter though, no paid killer. He didn't even carry a badge nowadays. He wanted to take his man all in one piece if possible, would only take him otherwise if he purely and definitely had to, as might be the case.

Daggart was a cunning and half-crazed killer as quick and slippery as a sidewinder. He had been hard to find. But Temperly had found him at last. Or thought he had. Temperly was a sort of detective after all but he wasn't always right and he himself would be the first to admit that. He had made mistakes. He had had to kill. He knew in his bones that he would, sometime, have to do that again.

If such was the case, a worthless scumhound like Daggart would be a prime candidate.

It had been a long trail. How would it pay off? Temperly looked up at the prime false front of the prime, garish whorehouse and asked himself that question.

Hell, Daggart could be watching him now from an upstairs window, wondering. Or Daggart could be miles away again, well-britched as he was and a free agent.

Temperly moved around to the establishment. He had left his neat brown stallion at the nearby livery stables. He had his rifle sloped at his side, his knife in the back of his belt, his handgun on his hip.

He was a tall, lean man with a long face and a crooked scar, like a dimple when he smiled, in his left cheek. His shoulders were wide and he carried himself loosely, moving quite neatly even in his high-heeled riding-boots.

As he passed into the shade of the alley which ran between the whorehouse and the place next door he pushed his hat to the back of his head. He had grey eyes and thick, long black hair bunched at the back, tendrilled at the sides.

It was late afternoon and he had seen men enter the garish establishment, but only a few. Big business would come later. Temperly couldn't wait for the time of big business, which wouldn't fit in with his plans anyway. Such plans! He smiled to himself and the scar on his cheek writhed.

It was quiet out back. There was an outside staircase. There was usually an outside staircase, which would feel many bootheels during the night. But now Temperly's heels made very little sound as he climbed.

Out back here the place was not, of course, as tall as the front. The garish false front. And now Temperly could see the long struts that held the false front up, protected the structure from the wind.

13

But as he climbed he could hear the building creaking like the stays of a fat old maid.

He reached the top and he could feel the wind building up, though it was not cold. Shouldn't like to come up here on a winter's night with a norther blowing, he thought. It was amazing what some men would go through just to get themselves pleasured by a willing young lady.

Had Daggart come up this way? Last night maybe. Temperly had told himself that he was now hot on the man's trail. He had gotten his latest info from an old-timer who had been robbed by Daggart and was lucky to be alive.

The vengeful man had told the pursuer that this town, which Temperly had never seen before, was Daggart's favourite place, that the outlaw had a favourite girl also in the bordello called Ranker's because it was run by a man and wife team named Bella and Carl Ranker. Temperly hadn't heard of them before, hadn't taken much of a shine to the town either. It had the appearance of a place where folks went to hide.

Or to visit Ranker's of course!

The door at the top of the outside staircase was not locked. Temperly opened it and slid his leanness through.

He was in a shadowed passage with doors on each side, about eight in all he figured.

One of those doors, next-door-but-one to where he was halted, opened almost soundlessly. He hooked his thumb in his belt very near to his gun.

A girl came through the door. She was stark naked, a thing of curves and shadows and smooth protuberances.

She saw him and stopped dead, half-turned towards him. She looked at him from a round, pretty face. A lock of yellowish hair obscured one eye. The other eye wore a gaze of coquettish challenge.

"Hallo, stranger," she said.

He thought she looked good enough

15

to eat. But right now he hadn't the time or the appetite.

"I didn't figure to disturb anybody, honey," he said. "I'm looking for a friend of mine. A feller called Daggart. Joe Daggart."

"Big man with a squint?" the girl asked.

"Yeh, that's him."

"He's Gaby's man. End of the passage. Door on the right."

"Thank you, precious. Catch you later, huh?"

She fluttered her eyelashes at him. "I'll be waiting," she said and turned back through the partially open door.

It closed softly behind her. Temperly wondered why she'd come through it in the first place, like she was and all. Naked as a plucked jaybird but a whole lot more wholesome.

He wondered whether he would actually see her again.

That could depend on what happened behind that other door at the end of the passage which he approached now.

And there was nothing but silence again. Was this establishment, the rooms anyway, soundproof or something?

All doors were closed, including the one he faced now as he halted. He was told nothing. He heard nothing.

★ ★ ★

"He ain't here," said the deputy, whose name was Jasper, Jas for short.

"Where is he then?" asked Silvo.

"Dunno. Ain't seen him this mornin'. Maybe he's still in bed."

"Why, was he sickening for somep'n y' think?" said Dooley.

"He was all right last night when he left me. I did a bit o' night duty an' should be at my bed now. But I'm still waitin' for the sheriff."

Jasper was far from stupid. He could figure from their attitudes, their strained expressions, that something bad had happened.

They told him quickly, baldly.

"God-a-mercy," he said.

17

He was a stocky, round-faced young man with thin, gingerish hair not unlike Dooley's but without a trace of grey.

He was still mighty young in many ways. He was shocked. "It's hardly believable," he said.

"It's believable and it happened," said Silvo harshly and Jasper looked at the silver-haired man oddly.

Silvo went on, "We want a posse an' we want it quick . . . "

"He's right," said Dooley. "We've gotta find Brake."

"All right."

The three went down the street, tried the main saloon and other like establishments. Nobody had seen Sheriff Oscar Brake. They went to the boarding-house where widower Oscar and other males resided. Even there nobody had seen him around.

The old gent in the room next to Oscar's said he had heard the lawman moving around a bit in there last night. But that was all.

"It's a goddam mystery," said Dooley.

2

TEMPERLY rapped on the door. Then he lowered the hand and tucked it in his belt in the spot were it was most comfortable, near the walnut butt of his short-barrelled Colt forty-four, a modified weapon which had been lovingly tended by an ancient gunsmith in San Antonio.

The door was opened slowly and not very wide. A comely female face peered out and its owner said, "I've got company, suh."

"I figure it's that company that I have to see on a matter of important business," said Temperly softly.

Behind the girl a deep voice growled, "Who the hell . . . ?"

Temperly pushed the door wide, tearing it away from the girl and shouldering past her.

The girl had on a flimsy shift which

didn't cover much of her. But Daggart was stark naked and he came off the bed like a big white fish with a black hairy pelt.

His big hands reached clawlike for the gunbelt and its contents across the back of the chair beside the bed. He was clumsy, but he was fast. Temperly was faster, though.

He covered the floor in two strides. His gun came out in a looping arc, round and over. The chunky steel barrel struck the big man on the crown of the head with a sound that could shake a man's teeth, driving Daggart down to the floor where he subsided with his face in the carpet.

The girl gasped and Temperly turned to her, pointed the gun at her. He raised his other hand, his forefinger uplifted in front of his pursed lips, and he said, "Sh-h-hhh . . . "

She stood still. She had red hair and a sharp, hard but not unattractive face. "Lie on the bed," the man said and her green eyes widened and her tongue

20

came out from her lips as if in some sort of anticipation.

She made a sort of shrugging motion and her shift slid away from her like loose skin and pooled on the floor and she was nude. She was sinuous and a mite heavy. Her movements were smooth as she lay on the bed in an inviting position.

Temperly grinned: he couldn't help it. He pulled the clothes up from the bottom of the bed and covered her with them, her face as well, hiding her completely.

From under there she made muffled, puzzled sounds. He bent close and stroked the shape of her face. "I can't stay right now, *chiquita*," he said. "I'm sorry. I want you to stay quiet like a mouse for a while. If you don't I might take umbrage, an' I'm not nice when I take umbrage."

He delved into his vest pocket and took out some greenbacks and peeled off a generous amount, rolled them into a spiral. He reached under the bedclothes and tucked the rich spiral between the girl's opulent breasts. He was gentle, letting his fingers linger.

The fingers went upwards then. He pulled the bedclothes down so that he could see her face. "I'm taking your friend Daggart with me," he said. "Do you mind?"

She shook her head slowly from side to side. She already had the roll of money in her hand, had slyly manipulated the bedclothes herself as he made his move. The hand with the money nestled between her breasts and her green eyes were filled with blatant invitation.

Temperly thought, don't these frails ever give up? He said, "Will you do what I say, honey? Quiet like a mouse, huh?"

She pouted. Then she said, "All right, suh, you can count on me."

Gently, he covered her up again. Daggart was beginning to make noises. Temperly didn't want him to start yelling. He took up the big man's gunbelt and slung it over his shoulder. He stood back from the bulk on the floor. Daggart could be a tricky bastard, maybe was playing possum. The noises he was making sounded hurtful and genuine, but Temperly wasn't taking any chances.

"I can hear you," he said. "You ain't hurt that bad."

There was blood on Daggart's sparsely-covered crown. He raised his head and there was a trickle of blood on the bovine features. The squinting eyes looked puzzled.

"You're Temperly," he said thickly. "Why you . . . ?"

"Cut it," interrupted the other man and jerked the short-barrelled Colt forty-four. "Get up. I don't want to shoot you here but I will if I have to."

Daggart lumbered to his feet. "I need my clobber."

It was in a heap at the bottom of the bed, a big slicker on top. With his free hand Temperly picked up the

23

slicker and slung it at Daggart.

"Put that on."

"I gotta . . . "

"That's all you're gettin', bucko. You ain't gonna catch cold."

Daggart shrugged into the long garment which was a bit ragged from wear. Temperly could smell it. But maybe that was just Daggart. There were bordello fragrances, but this was different.

"My boots . . . "

"You don't need no boots. March!"

There was no sound from the bed. Daggart hadn't even looked in that direction. His squint eyes watched Temperly warily now.

"Move! March!"

"You won't get away with this," said the big man. But he took his gaze away, and he marched.

They went down the outside back staircase and didn't see a soul. Temperly steered the barefoot slicker-clad man along the back of the town and to the livery stables.

24

The aged hostler, having already figured the tall, lean rider for a lawman, didn't seem too surprised to see them. Temperly jerked a thumb. "Where's his horse?"

"Here, suh." A jerked thumb from the oldster. He got the rawboned grey nag, the saddle. He watched the big man being forced to mount and he grinned. Evidently he didn't take much to the big feller.

He accepted the extra money that Temperly offered and said, "Pleasant journey," and gave a little cackle.

They rode out of town. They saw a few folk but nobody seemed to pay them much heed.

It's been kind of easy after all, Temperly reflected. Almost too easy!

"I oughta had my hat," grumbled Daggart.

"You don't need no hat."

"It's getting hot. I might fall to sunstroke or somep'n."

Temperly had no further comment to make on the subject then. He made his prisoner ride ahead of him.

Daggart kept complaining, even uttering bloodcurdling threats.

Finally Temperly threw the man a bandanna and told him to wrap his head in it and stuff one end in his mouth. Leastways, if he didn't want to get slugged again and spend the rest of his journey tied face down across his saddle.

Temperly had thought of tying the man's hands behind him, his feet under the horse's belly. But he didn't want Daggart falling, being dragged maybe. If Temperly could get Daggart to their destination all in one piece he would do just that. But if he had to shoot the large, useless son-of-a-bitch he was fully capable of doing that thing instead.

He had eliminated scum before. But it gave him a sense of sardonic satisfaction to do things the other way and leave somebody else — a judge, a jury, a hangman — to fix the harder part. He figured Daggart for a lethal necktie anyway.

He had come prepared. They rested. He fed his prisoner and watered him. The trail was long and sparse. They didn't see many people and people weren't curious.

Daggart complained, as he would, of a sore ass.

"That's the least of your troubles, bucko," his captor told him.

It was dark when they saw the lights of the ranch that was their destination. There was a town the other side of it. They hadn't touched the town.

"You made your mark on this territory, didn't you?" Temperly said.

"I don't recognize anything around here. I ain't been here before."

"No, only once maybe, just long enough to kill a man over a game of poker and light out with the winnings," said Temperly. He reflected that he hadn't bothered to check what *dinero* Daggart had had with him. Well, the redheaded frail called Gaby was welcome to it! "

Riders came out to meet them.

27

They joshed the big man savagely for his nakedness and one of them said they should swing him in the breeze right off. But that wasn't the way it was meant to be done. Not yet anyway. But they took the slicker from him and threw it in the grass and made him ride the rest of the way in the buff. Cal Temperly made no objection.

The rancher was waiting for them. He saw that the prisoner was supplied with shirt and pants and a tattered pair of moccasins. But he would not look at the big squint-eyed man or speak to him.

Daggart had another journey ahead of him, but Temperly's job was finished. He took the money from the rancher, the pay for bringing the man in, the man who had killed the rancher's brother across a poker-table. A wanted man. The rancher asked about the reward. But he only got the answer he'd expected.

The lean, grey-eyed hunter said he

was no bounty-chaser, the money could maybe be given to the local school or hospital or something. He left the ranch. He skirted the town. He had in mind another town, and a girl, not very far away.

She ran a little stores left to her by her parents who had both died during the epidemic of sickness in a particularly terrible winter a couple of years ago.

In the small hours she ran her man a hot soapy bath and she laved his back then left him to soak in the deep tub. But she returned and had a paper in her hand.

"The telegraph man brought it," she said softly.

She had big blue eyes and corn-coloured hair and she was a quiet person for a restless man.

"I suppose you'll have to be riding again," she said, but there was no reproach in her voice.

"We'll see," he said.

He did not give her a complete

answer until they were in bed in the early morning and had completed a long and extremely pleasurable period of love-making.

"The message was from Silvo. You remember Silvo, don't you, Tansy?"

"I remember Silvo. Who could forget Silvo? A dangerous man."

"That he is. But not a completely bad one. He asks for my help."

"He's been of help to you in the past, hasn't he?"

"Yes, he has."

"Then you'll have to be of help to him now, won't you?"

"That's the way it is, Tansy."

"I know. So be it then. Get some rest now while you can, my heart."

It was her favourite endearment. He had never heard it from anybody else, never wanted to.

She, after all, was asleep before he was. He dozed. And he remembered Silvo.

He remembered the last time he had been involved with Silvo. In a breezy town called Wildwind. A murderous conspiracy. A mystery . . .

Silvo wasn't good on mysteries. Silvo needed another mind, another gun maybe . . .

3

THE townsfolk knew. They had the right to know.

Deputy Jas (everybody called him that) had been desperately looking for his chief, helped it seemed by the enigmatic Silvo and his old friend Dooley. But nobody had seen Sheriff Oscar Brake where they might've been expected to see him. Or anyplace else for that matter.

The rumours grew. But many folks had the tale right by now. The Jolen family had been slaughtered in a horrific way. As if Injuns had been there. But there weren't many Injuns in this territory now, and those that hung around were tame ones.

Men still ranged around the edge of town, the town called Garrington, and further out. But life and work and business had to go on. The women didn't go far from their homes and the kids at school were watched.

Men tried not to ride alone. But more than one — bunches here and there — went seeking the missing lawman, and didn't find him. And gave up.

It was said that old Oscar could look after himself. Was he a man alone anyway? His deputy didn't know. Nobody knew. Leastways, nobody said they knew anything . . .

Presently Deputy Jas left with Silvo and Dooley. Too much time had been wasted. And, with his boss absent, the deputy was in charge now.

The town waited. Then the three men returned with a buckboard, three shrouded bodies upon it.

A posse might have been in order then. But what could a posse look for?

The bodies were laid in the under-taking parlour. Folks came to look, filing in silently, and then turning away with sickness, sadness, outrage.

Rumours began to grow.

All kinds of rumours and speculation. And suspicion.

It was no wonder that all kinds of feelings got mixed up when at last Deputy Jas did take out a volunteer bunch on posse and Silvo and Dooley stayed in town. The enigmatic, silver-haired dark young man in the dark clothing, and his jokey, cynical, elderly sidekick.

They were watched. And twilight came and the posse hadn't returned.

Then, though, Silvo and Dooley rode out and there was a great uncertainty. But nobody followed them.

There was surprise when they returned after an absence of only about ten minutes or so and they had another rider with them, a stranger on a neat brown stallion.

The saloon was still open and the three men entered it. The stranger was of about the same age as Silvo, give or take a year or so. They seemed to know each other well.

The stranger was lean, but taller than

the almost dapper silver-haired Silvo.

The stranger wasn't as dark-complexioned as Silvo but saturnine notwithstanding and with a crooked scar on one cheek.

Folks greeted Silvo and Dooley, gave the new man small glances. Some said they thought they might have seen him before. Others were sure they hadn't. He wasn't introduced to anybody and he joined his two companions and took a bottle and glasses, and all three of them moved to an empty table in a corner.

And, over in another corner, an old-timer said to an equally elderly friend, "That's Cal Temperly."

"The gunfighter?"

"You could call him that, I guess. But he's a man of many sorts."

★ ★ ★

It was twilight when the members of the posse saw the vultures wheeling in the sky, saw them only as drifting, almost ghostly shapes. But they heard the querulous cries. Those ugly birds didn't like to see humans moving on their horses, the whole bunch obviously very much alive.

"No shooting," said Jas. "There's somep'n dead there, but there could be live ones too."

The obscene birds wheeled away. The light was not good and there was a shifting quality about the bundle of odd-shaped rocks ahead as the men and horses approached them, and Jas dismounted and the others followed suit.

Guns were drawn and, at Jas's signal, the men spread out. The young deputy knew what he was about.

Then: "Here," hissed somebody.

Soon they were all gathered around the body in the central hollow among the rocks.

"Oscar," said Jas and went down on one knee beside the still form.

The body had no eyes but the vultures hadn't had time to do much more damage. It looked as if the body had been partially buried in the loose soil of the dip and the birds had had to do some digging, squabbling among themselves as they did this.

Between the bloody eye-sockets and a little above them was another, smaller, red hole, dirt caked around it. Sheriff Oscar Brake had been shot in the head at close range. Subsequent examination revealed that the gun had been so close that its bullet had torn through the big man's temple and brains and taken part of the back of his head away. This hadn't been a stand-up killing, it had been a cold-blooded execution.

Men turned away, began ranging. They were as quiet as possible. They made small sounds, as so did the horses. The light was getting worse and the beasts were a mite restive. They smelled death in the soughing wind. But there didn't seem to be anything around and beyond this small arena of execution and a man was able to say softly, "I've found somep'n."

It was a small over-and-under pocket pistol of indeterminate gender which had become lodged between two boulders. One of its twin muzzles was black and ragged, had been torn apart. There was still a bullet in the other barrel.

"Anybody who tried to use that now would like to blow his goddam hand off," hissed the man who had found it.

Jas said, "Looks like somebody dropped it and it went off in the rocks, was useless, an' he left it there. That was a mite careless of him mebbe." He took the weapon from the man and tucked it in the front of his belt.

"Careful," said somebody. "You don't want to blow away any of that prime equipment o' yourn."

But this was not a time of jollity. There were grim things to be about. "We've got to take Oscar home," somebody said.

Jas said, "God, it's gettin' darker.

Almost as if a storm's brewing. I wish we could see more, we might even be able to pick up some sorta trail from here."

"We ain't seen any kind of a trail yet," said a man. "And if it hadn't been for them birds we wouldn't have found Oscar."

"They should've buried him deeper," said somebody else.

"Mebbe that's another small mistake they made," said Jas.

"Was it the same folk who did that to the Jolens?" It was a fruitless half-question from another posse-member, his words dying on the still air.

"We'll take Oscar home," said Jas. "We'll come back tomorrow an' see if we can pick somep'n up. Hope it doesn't rain . . . Let's get him up. Gently. *Gently*."

Later, a bunch of them gathered in the Garrington schoolhouse. Among them then were Dooley and Silvo, and the latter's newly-arrived friend, who was introduced as Cal Temperly.

Deputy Jas said he had heard Sheriff Oscar speak of Cal Temperly, and Temperly said he remembered Oscar from the old days. But he didn't enlarge on this, not forgetting however to commiserate with the young deputy over the loss of his chief, his friend.

The old-timer who had first identified Temperly in the saloon was also present at the meeting. His name was Silas Tripp and he had been a lawyer, and even a judge.

He was one of the town's elders. He had a proposal to put forward and the others listened to him with respect, if, here and there, a measure of doubt . . .

4

"THEY hadn't taken any of his clothes," said Jas. "And why would they anyway? But they obviously took his horse, an' that'ud be natural, wouldn't it? Oscar always had a good horse. And they took his rifle, his gunbelt, Colt, ammunition, his knife . . . "

"But the busted pistol wasn't his?" put in Temperly.

"No. Never saw it before."

Temperly had the little gun now. He hadn't tried to fire it, might have lost his hand had he done this. But he'd managed, with his wicked-looking knife, to get the remaining shot out of the second barrel, the comparatively undamaged one.

He took the derringer now from the back of his belt where it had nestled next to the pouched big knife.

"It was a natty little weapon," he said. "Somebody must've been proud of it."

Although the front of the gun was blackened and torn, the butt was comparatively unmarked and was of warm yellow bone chased with silver, with a silver loop at the bottom so that the weapon could be hung from a hook or a swivel if its owner liked such fancies, the lethal little toy dangling for all to see.

"Could be a custom-built job," Temperly said. He handled the gun as if he knew all sorts, had handled all sorts. He weighted the little pistol in his hand and eyed it thoughtfully as if he thought it might tell him something. But then, abruptly, he returned it to the back of his belt.

Temperly and the deputy rode a little ahead of the others, among whom were Silvo and Dooley. Everybody knew now that it was Silvo who had sent for Temperly. And town elder, Silas Tripp, had carried it on from there.

Temperly was now marshal of the smallish but thriving township of Garrington, not a political post, but a temporary honorary one. Deputy Jasper, who had taken a shine to the lean man, spoken of very highly by his late boss, Oscar Brake, had gone along with the proposal, had accepted Temperly as chief and ally.

The new marshal didn't even wear a badge. But he was the boss-man now and he carried that authority as if it was something he was well used to. Everybody else had gone along, or had seemed to do just that.

"I'll scout," the new marshal said and he moved away from Jas, moved onwards.

Silvo came forward, his shining silver-white locks blowing a little in the morning breeze. He went past the deputy and caught up with Temperly.

"You got somep'n to tell me?" the lean man asked.

"Nope. I see you've still got the ol' pigsticker."

"Yeh, I have."

"It's a grand ol' knife. A sort of nearly bowie, huh?"

"I guess."

"Bet it'd make a dandy throwing-knife."

"Has been," said Temperly.

Laconic rejoinders: like old times.

Temperly remembered how he had killed a man with that knife. In a town called Wildwind.[1]

That had been some job-o'-work, that had!

And Silvo had come along at the end of it. When the battle began — *and ended*.

And now here was Silvo again.

Like old times. Yeh! Or was it?

The weather was sultry. There was a small breeze but that was not cooling at all. It was like a breath of hell. The morning was still early. There had been

_____

[1] *See the novel 'Wildwind'*

44

sun but now there was none and the humidity made sweat pop from a man's skin and caused the horses to breathe hard and labour.

There had been no rain in this territory for a long time. Yesterday it had seemed that there might be. Old-timers had predicted it but it hadn't come.

Now, wiping his face with a soiled bandanna, one of the riders remarked that it was gonna be a humdinger of a day.

As if these words betokened some kind of signal, the sun began to blaze and men and horses laboured more and the men swore.

But none of it lasted long, for a black cloud appeared and swept across the sky and blotted out the sun. There was greyness, and then there was blackness and, with dramatic suddenness, the rain came. It poured, and then with malicious spite under its skirts, it became a deluge.

There was the wind too, blustering

from a distance, then coming closer with a sort of monotonous roar; and forked lightning lit the veritable darkness in spiteful bursts, and thunder, that had at first rolled, exploded like cannonballs.

Men struggling with slickers had them almost blown from their hands, but luckily, maybe manfully, nobody actually lost one of the floppy garments and soon the riders looked like spirits battling the elements on ghost horses; and they were losing . . .

Their destination, the place that Deputy Jasper was leading them to, was not far ahead now. The rock outcrops and, beyond them, the low range of hills. They couldn't be seen now, but they were there.

It was as if the storm, the complete, furious elements, were conspiring, with evil intent, to keep them from their destination, to destroy them even, leaving them as sodden carcases in the swimming ground, their sightless dead eyes staring at the unreached shelter as the sun came up again and bathed the hills with mocking golden rays.

It was impossible to ride any more. The men dismounted from their horses and led them. The beasts were fractious. The thunder and lightning and the lashing rain scared even the hardiest and most seasoned of them, the old-stagers, not long in the tooth but long in experience with one rider, a man they trusted.

But the men were scared also and their feelings were communicated to the canny animals. They were all being attacked by an elemental fury that was past understanding.

The men had seen violent storms before, with or without the dubious companionship of sometimes fractious horseflesh. But many of the riders said afterwards — and that wasn't only the young ones — that they'd never experienced a storm quite like this one before.

A man stumbled on tufted sodden ground and came too near one of his horse's hooves. The beast was startled and lashed out, catching its rider on the side of the head and plunging him to the ground. He passed out. The horse ran wildly into the driving rain and soon disappeared.

The galloping runaway was instrumental in bringing to the other men's notice the state of his erstwhile rider, who now was unconscious in the wet grass and the mud. He was lifted up and placed across the saddle of another horse, whose owner tried to staunch the blood from his wounded *compadre's* temple, pink in the running rain and very nasty.

They reached the very rocks that they had sought. Jas's guidance had been good and, after the rain started, the thing to do had been just to battle on in as straight a line as they could with Jas in the lead again, accompanied by Temperly, Silvo and Dooley.

The men tried to gentle the horses, make them stay. But another one broke away and fled into the rain, his shouting rider pursuing, his words destroyed by the wind. Both man and horse disappeared, and the rider's comrades, while trying to hold their own mounts, peered anxiously.

The man, unmounted, reappeared like a wet gargoyle and staggered back to the rocks and fell to the ground. He was unhurt but completely exhausted.

There was a meagre shelter among the rocks, but it was better that nothing, and men and beasts tried to make the most of it, the horses now too tired to run any more it seemed, and the men definitely at the end of their tether.

Still the elements sought them out with malicious glee, however, and if frustrated now, with a growing fury. *Murderous*. Here in this rocky outcrop adjacent to the foothills which now couldn't be seen except when lightning flashed, the tattered body of Sheriff Oscar Brake had been found.

The hollow where the body had been was full of rainwater now and there were no vultures. None of the men had paused to speculate where those obscene birds could be now.

Deputy Jasper tried to shout above the clamorous fury of the storm, but nobody heard what he was trying to tell them. He desisted, hung his head, the rain running down his face and dripping from the brim of his hat. A sudden shaft of lightning briefly illuminated that face and it looked very young.

But the shouting elements had no respect for humankind, or for animal kind for that matter, and the storm continued unabated for another half-hour or so, though it seemed longer to the crouching men, the drooping beasts.

One man checked the time with his gunmetal hunter held in the dubious shelter of his slicker as the storm finally and slowly abated.

A thin drizzle remained, falling from the heavens in a melancholy fashion. And then through this veil of wet, a watery sun began to shine. Ignoring the rain now, and compared to the past fury of the storm it was little more than a veil of sodden mist, the men raised themselves up and squinted against the sun.

It got brighter, and the small rain ceased and the men's clothes steamed as they began to dry.

There was no trail and although the grass now shone in a welter of brown and green, everybody knew that any passage would be soggy and difficult. The ground had been bone-hard and farmers had prayed for rain. The mocking elements had given them more than they bargained for and much of the ground now would be like a quagmire.

The posse had lost two horses, which might or might not turn up again. They had a wounded man who was unconscious now and moaning. They had to get him back to town and medical attention.

They gave up their abortive search and wended their sodden and weary way back, two of the horses double-laden. Progress was slow but they reached the town and were somewhat peeved to be greeted only with tales of woe about what the storm had done to property and chattels and even to a few luckless people.

No fatalities though, and that was a mercy. The doc looked at the rider who'd been kicked in the head and said he wasn't about to die either. The man's horse had turned up and was browsing contentedly in the livery stables. The other runaway cayuse never came back. Maybe the lightning got him, or he joined a wild bunch, of which there were a few, of the sort that horse-dealer Dooley loved to chase and tame.

5

BY the following morning Temperly and Silvo had left the town of Garrington once more. The night before, Dooley had gone back to his little horse-ranch where, while he was away, there was only an old Mexican *vaquero* in charge.

By the morning the rain had finished completely and there was pale sunshine, and a few early risers saw the new deputy, Silvo and his old friend the marshal, ride out together in the direction they had taken yesterday, the direction the posse had taken.

It was said that maybe they were on their way to pick up Dooley, as those three seemed to make up a tight trio, a team.

Deputy Jas was around later. He was kind of close-mouthed and if he knew where the marshal was heading, didn't let on. He was in charge, of course, while the boss-man was absent. He gave the same loyalty to Temperly it seemed that he had to his late friend and chief Oscar Brake.

There would be a funeral soon. Poor Sheriff Brake would be laid to rest. Nobody knew whether Temperly and Silvo would be back for that.

Dooley's Mexican hand, Pablo, turned up with his wagon to get some supplies. He said his boss was back there working with a fractious mare. They hadn't had any visitors that day, hadn't seen anybody at all.

By that time Temperly and Silvo were many miles away from Garrington. They had visited again the spot where Sheriff Brake's body had been found. The sun was getting hotter and everything was drying up.

"I guess we need even more rain to really soak the land," Silvo had said.

The hollow where Brake's body had lain was dry except for a puddle at its bottom. The rocks shone in the sun. Temperly, obviously uninterested in the weather right now, was looking at the little broken derringer that had been found not far from the corpse of the murdered lawman.

He said, "That wound in Brake's head could've been made by this weapon and the show-off bastard who fired that one shot could've just reloaded the one chamber when he dropped his goddam derringer and it went off."

Silvo chuckled humourlessly, said, "Mebbe he shot his own balls off."

Temperly seemed to take this remark seriously. "Weren't no blood," he said.

"The show-off bastard left his derringer where it lay."

"Weren't no good to him anymore."

You'd have thought he'd keep it for a souvenir."

"I'm glad he didn't. When he dropped it they were moving out this way after leaving the body, after taking Brake's horse and all his accoutrements."

"Looks that way." Silvo pointed. "So

you think they went in that direction, huh?"

"'Pears that way, wouldn't you say?"

"I guess."

"That damn' rain was no help, no help at all. But we'll look thataways, pardner, what do you say?" Temperly was mounting up. Silvo followed suit.

They were back on the trail again, hopefully, professionally. Riding slowly, scanning the ground. Dismounting. Finding nothing. Going on as the sun got hotter in a way that seemed to presage a dry, blazing day.

They had tucker and water with them but, not knowing yet where the trail might lead them, they kept on saving it as long as they could. They were taking a drink from their canteens though, when, gazing about him as he sipped, Silvo said, "If we go in a straight line there's a town ahead called Poison Creek. Little more'n a settlement last time I was here . . ."

"Strange name for a town of any kind," put in Temperly.

"Yeh, the creek which runs past it was supposed to be poisoned. Came from a spring. Water had a hellish bitter taste an' gave folks stomach cramps. Then folks dammed it somehow, sort of relocated the creek, and the water ain't so bad now so I've been told. Drinkable anyway. But I reckon only a few folk who have no place else to go stay here for any length of time. Settlers. But a lot o' drifters."

"A place to call in at if you want somep'n, huh, an' ain't aiming to take up permanent residence?"

"That's about it."

"Let's take a looksee then."

"There was a trading-post," said Silvo.

There still was. They found it.

It was easy to find, easy to see, situated as it was on the nearside of the narrow creek as the two riders approached it. On the other side of the creek the shacks spread out higgledy-piggledy, the whole set out in a blazing

57

sunshine that did nothing to hide its faults.

This was no ambitious township like Garrington. This was a sinkhole. Silvo said it hadn't changed, that the trading-post in fact looked even more dilapidated than it had when he'd last visited it.

Then he saw the man behind the counter and he said, "It's the same geezer."

An amazingly tall individual — unless, hidden by the counter, he was standing on a box; which didn't prove to be the case. And amazingly thin also, a beanpole with a small almost hairless human head perched atop it like a well-skinned, dried up pumpkin.

But eyes, caught by the sunlight in that pale hairless face, shrewd and appraising. Not an old man, though older than his two visitors, but with eyes that appeared to have seen a lot, eyes that couldn't mistake the stripe of these two.

The taller, leaner one with the strange

dimpled scar on his cheek who, though he wore no badge, carried himself with an undeniable air of authority. Probably a lawman of some kind anyway . . . And his companion, having a sort of familiar look about him. A dangerous one. They were both dangerous. But had the second one been alone the beanpole proprietor would've taken him for a gunfighter, a bounty-hunter maybe.

Maybe they were both bounty-hunters after all!

"Welcome, gents," said the beanpole in a high, thin voice, coming as it did from way up there. "What can I pleasure you with?"

A strange way to put it. But maybe beanpole had a couple of girls stashed in back.

Silver hair, he thought, shining in the sun like the real precious stuff. Dark clothing; big black hat. Then he remembered the name. Of course! *Silvo*.

And it was Silvo who said, "Coffee, my friend. And a couple of o' them special bottles you keep in ice back o'that counter."

"There speaks a wise man," said beanpole. "Gents, you couldn't do better on a scorcher of a day like this'n."

Over his shoulder he yelled, "Coffee."

The voice that answered was as thin as his own but undeniably feminine. The man bent and delved under the bar and came up with two slim bottles of beer that dripped with moisture.

"Known far an' wide," he said. "Far an' wide. Coldest drink this side o' the Yukon. Set a while, gents. Settle up 'fore you go. Can I mebbe get you somep'n to eat?"

The two men exchanged glances. Temperly nodded. Silvo asked, "What've you got?"

The tall cadaverous man brought from under the counter a tattered ledger and flipped through the pages, left the book open at one, turned it towards the visitors.

"We can do any o' that today. A

small wait if you gents don't mind. My missus is a prime cook. Real prime. But she don't like bein' rushed."

"Understandable," said Temperly and bent his head next to Silvo's.

They had both taken their hats off and the black hair and the silver made a striking contrast. They both stabbed a finger down in the same place.

"I commend you gents," said the tall man. "You chose right well. That's a set 'un that is famed far an' wide. Pardon me for a few moments, won't you." He turned, disappeared through a curtain.

"Right affable, ain't he?" said Silvo out of the corner of his mouth.

"A salesman all right," said Temperly.

"I heard him an' his missus ran a theatre troupe 'fore they settled here," said Silvo.

"It figures," said Temperly.

An uncorked bottle each, the plum-coloured glass cold to their fingers, they sucked like hungry babies. "Goes down right well," said Silvo, and turning

61

about, Temperly, unspeaking, following his example.

There was an arrogance about them.

There were four other men in the long narrow room with the counter at one side, the door and the window at the other. The place was cluttered with all kinds of goods, leaning against the walls, hanging from the walls, stacked on the floor.

There were three round tables, ten chairs and two stools, none of which were at the counter. The four men sat at a table by the window, had watched the newcomers approach and come in. They weren't being surreptitious at all now either. They stared back at the strangers. Arrogance didn't faze that bunch, nossir, not atall-atall.

Out of the corner of his mouth (he was good at that) Silvo said, "Border scum."

The proprietor came out with two steaming mugs of coffee.

"If you will choose a table, gents, your meals will be brought out to you as soon as possible."

They took the coffees to the table nearest the counter and over to the side a bit. The bunch by the window watched them with sullen interest. The two parties could see each other well. There had been nothing accidental or sloppy about the two strangers' choice of table.

The lady who brought their meals to them was a surprise to them both. Silvo said that though he had seen the man before, he certainly hadn't seen this lady or he would've remembered her. She was evidently the proprietor's missus. She was younger than him. No chicken — but a pippin.

She wore a flowered apron tied tightly at the waist and showing off a good figure. She walked with a sort of flowing gait as if, Temperly said afterwards, she was strolling onto a lighted stage to the acclaim of thousands. Beneath her apron her long dress almost swept the boards. She had good ankles.

Her hair was long and black, set in

long waves. There were wings of grey over her ears, heightening the theatrical aspect of her whole demeanour. Her features were patrician, though finely lined and, as she appraised the two men, her eyes were a bright blue like those of a curious young girl.

"Gentlemen," she said.

They both half rose, said, "Ma'am."

She laid out the food.

6

THEY had brown chicken with frankfurters and chili, but not too much of the latter, and a mixture of vegetables and small sliced onions. The dish gave off an appetizing smell that was hard to describe. Silvo said the taste matched the smell. There was more coffee and then deep-dish pie which seemed to consist of apples and plums, plus other succulent berries and the added subtle flavours of spices.

The two men leaned back well content and smoked and the lady came in to collect the dishes and Silvo said, "That was mighty prime, ma'am."

"Excellent," said Temperly. "Excellent."

"Thank you, gentlemen."

The boys in the corner had watched all this. They didn't seem to have had any food, but they had certainly been imbibing. And they were getting louder.

One of them made a loud remark in which the word 'filly' occurred, but neither Temperly or Silvo heard the gist of it. It was evidently aimed at the woman though, and they didn't like that. She was on her way to the back again, carrying her tray, and there was no pause in her beautiful progress.

But now the group by the window were like a bunch of jackasses guffawing to split their sides.

"Scum," said Silvo, very mildly.

That was a bad sign.

"We're here for a purpose, *amigo*," said Temperly. "Don't get side-tracked."

"Is that what you call it?" said Silvo, softly.

The laughter died to a sort of mindless spluttering. The two men had taken full notice of the four and Silvo's succinct description of them had been very apt. They were dirty and ragged and hairy, their very appearance calculated to strike terror into beholders: smallholders, peaceful townsfolk unchaperoned females and the like. Scum like those four preyed on the weak and helpless. They were human but they were worse than the wild predators, the animals whose nature it was to hunt and kill.

Temperly and Silvo wondered whether, as the woman had brought the food to the table, that had been the first view the bunch by the window had had of her. The two old friends now studiously ignored the bunch. The tall proprietor stood behind his counter again. Afer coming back he hadn't seemed to be moving much.

An old man came in and was greeted by him, bought tobacco, looked nervously at the bunch by the window, shuffled out again. One of the bunch said something about an 'old goat' and there was more ribald laughter.

"They're spoiling for trouble," said Silvo.

Temperly gave a long sigh. "I guess," he said, nothing more.

"It's a quiet time," said the tall proprietor suddenly from behind Temperly and Silvo.

They both turned their heads, and Silvo said, "I guess it is."

The bunch by the window obviously heard the small exchange. It was a signal for more raucous merriment, with a nasty flavour which seemed to literally seep into the air and despoil the other mixed and not so unpleasant odours.

But then, suddenly, their heads bent forward over the table, the bunch by the window seemed to be arguing among themselves and one of them was heard to say, "Let's get going." But not one of them rose right then.

Silvo said, "I'm thinking that this is a strange setting for a trading-post with a couple like those two," he jerked his head in the direction of the counter, the back, "a woman who looks — an' cooks — the way that woman does."

The dark man had lowered his voice so that neither the man behind the counter or the arguing boys by the window could possibly hear his words.

Temperly said, "I guess this place does good with passing pilgrims though, has a name for good gear, good service, good grub."

"Yeh," said Silvo. Momentarily he had seemed to forget the existence of the bunch by the window. But now they were getting mighty noisy again as if they didn't mean to be ignored.

A chair went over with a clatter, and one of the boys was on his feet. And he was a big one.

He didn't stand quite as tall as the man behind the counter but he was much bulkier. He was much dirtier too, dirty all over, and looked about as menacing as a grizzly on the prod. Temperly and Silvo just had to look at him.

"Oh my," said Temperly.

But it seemed that right now this particular member of the border bunch was not paying any attention to the two strangers, was hardly aware of them any more, was treating them with contempt.

He marched past them and started to go through the trap at the end of the counter.

"Hold it," said the man behind the counter and, watching with interest, Temperly and Silvo saw that the beanpole had a sawn-off shotgun and it was pointed straight at the interloper's big belly.

The big man stopped dead and looked at the beanpole with the menacing gun and said petulantly, "I just wanted to pay my respects to the lovely lady."

"Turn about and leave my stores," said the beanpole in his high, carrying actor's voice. "And take your three friends with you. I don't want to see any of you in here again."

The dirty giant squinted, seemed at a loss for words. He was a very dangerous simpleton though, that was very, very evident.

The next voice that spoke came from

the other side of the room and it said, "Drop the shotgun, mister, or you're gonna be full o' lead."

All eyes were drawn to the window then, as they would have to be. The other three members of the border bunch were on their feet and two of them had guns drawn and pointing.

The third, who stood a little away from the table and to one side, had his thumbs hooked into the front of his belt. He was younger than his companions but, in some subtle way, appeared to be the leader.

He had long dark hair and a Mexican hat, though he wasn't all that Mexican. He had cold blue eyes and a twisted smile which seemed to be pasted on his still, sallow poker face.

The beanpole behind the counter didn't actually drop the shotgun but placed it carefully on the clear expanse of wood before him.

The young leader said, "Big Ed allus gets like this when he's had a mite too much to drink. Then he's just got to

have him a woman. We can do nothin'
with him till he's had a woman. He's
taken quite a fancy to your lady, an'
I can't say I blame him."

The voice was husky and the small
twisted smile was evil and the voice
rose, saying, "Step back a little, Ed,
an' let the gentleman out where we
can see him. An' then you go in back
an' do your business. But don't take
too long, mind."

"I won't, Lenny," said the giant like
an obedient talking hound.

"You can't . . . " began the beanpole.
And the young man called Lenny cut
him short.

"Do like you're told or we'll shoot
you anyway and nobody ull' look after
your lady then, will they?"

"We might," said Cal Temperly.
"Me an' my pardner here."

7

THEY were both on their feet and had stepped away from their chairs and from each other. There was a sizeable gap between them.

"I'll take half o'that all right," said the dark man with the long silver hair.

"Don't be loco, pilgrims," said young Lenny with the big hat.

The stately dark-haired woman came through the curtain behind the counter as if making a grand entrance, the star of the show. It was a gallant entrance made all the more effective by the fact that she had a levelled long-barrelled pistol — looked like a Remington forty-four.

Her husband saw her and opened his mouth as if to say something. But no sound came. And he grabbed his shotgun from the top of the counter and swung it around as Big Ed reached for his gun.

One barrel of the sawn-off went like a cannon-blast under the low roof and the giant went backwards on his heels and over, hit the floor hard, his weapon sliding back into its holster.

"Carla," shrilled the tall man, dropping his shotgun again; and he grabbed his wife and pulled her down with him.

Shots winged over their heads. But now the bunch by the door had fired at the wrong people and they had missed. And they had lost their edge.

Without even a sign passing between them, yet operating like a team, Temperly and Silvo had drawn their weapons. Half-crouching, guns levelled like pointing fingers, they thumbed hammers.

The two men with the smoking guns over by the window were both hit. One of them went backwards, his head smashing into the window, the glass breaking like a spiteful echo of the gunshots.

The other fell across the table on his belly and sprawled, his dark eyes staring. His mate had slid, and sat now against the wall beneath the window and clutched his breast with both hands as blood burst through his clutching fingers.

The boy called Lenny got his gun out. He was fast, but there was a look of shocked surprise on his lean rat-face and he wasn't smooth enough; his gun jerked, didn't come high enough. He got a shot off but it was wide. Then two bullets hit him, not a pin to put between them, and Lenny caught them fully. His gun flew from his hand and clattered to the floor and he went through the shattered window, kicking his dying partner in the face in the process.

The echoes died, but the room was still full of black smoke and the pungent smell of it; and the blossoming sickening odour of battle and of death.

"God-almighty," said the tall proprietor, leaning on his counter now. He had his sawn-off shotgun in his hands again. Like a man in a trance he put it gently down on the warm wood.

Then he looked back a little and down and, as before, he called out his wife's name. But his high voice rose to a near-screech now.

"Carla! *Carla*!"

And, as Temperly and Silvo turned, the proprietor's lanky frame disappeared wholly behind the counter and his voice wailed wordless questions. And, as if in mockery, the dying man beneath the shattered window whined and whistled in his dying struggles.

Temperly and Silvo moved. The bloodstained dead hulk of Big Ed lay across the counter-trap and this was ajar. The giant had forced it partially open as he fell and the boards around it were slippery with his blood.

Temperly and Silvo could see the woman's skirts as she lay on the other side of the counter. She was very still.

Then her man moved closer towards her and, at the same time, the two other men dragged Big Ed's body out of the way.

Temperly pushed the trap wider and moved through and Silvo gingerly followed him.

"Let me," said Temperly and the tall thin man dazedly moved aside.

Temperly bent over the woman. There was blood in her lush black hair and red spider-trickles ran down one side of her face which was very white. Her eyes were squinched tightly shut as if great pain had struck her. But she was still alive.

"Nasty crease across the top of her head," said Temperly. "Must've been the shot that boy fired, wild, came through the trap an' got her."

"Can we . . . ?"

"Yeh, help me pick her up."

Between them Temperly and the woman's husband carried her in back and placed her on the couch. She began to moan, her eyes flickering.

From behind the two men, Silvo said, "She'll be all right. I'll check out here." He went back through the curtain.

When he returned, the other two were helping the woman to sit up. She was dazed but trying to smile. The colour was coming back into her face from which her husband had cleaned the blood. She was a very handsome female and Silvo's eyes appraised the fact. But then he looked at Temperly and said, "That boy's still alive but only just."

Temperly left the married couple and followed Silvo across the shop and through the door. The boy Lenny had managed to prop himself against the wall outside beside the shattered window. The sun was in his face and his eyes were closed.

"He's gone," said Silvo.

Temperly got down on one knee and looked into the young border drifter's face. Then the eyes slowly opened.

Temperly took the fancy broken derringer from his belt and held it in front of the pale blue eyes in which a modicum of life still flickered.

"This yours, bucko? Do you know this?"

The eyes looked at the small thing with the ornate bone and silver-chased butt and the blackened barrel. They were eyes that, though so young, knew weapons, and this was the last weapon they would see.

The twisted lips opened and one word came out, croaking, halting.

"No-o-oo . . . "

The head shook from side to side and then it drooped upon the bloodied breast.

The wide-brimmed Mexican hat lay on the young man's knee. Silvo picked it up and placed it on Lenny's head, pulled it down over his face, said, "They do say that dying folk allus tell the truth. I guess this one did."

"I'm inclined to think you're right," said Temperly. "We got the wrong bunch, *amigo*."

"Sure. But they had to be got, didn't

they? They'd have killed us, Temp, and that feller back there. And the woman when they'd finished with her."

"I guess they would."

Folks were coming out of shacks and tentatively approaching the narrow creek at the other side of which the trading-post stood. Temperly went to the edge of the creek and, hands hooked in the front of his belt, looked across at them. They halted.

"It's all right, folks," the lean man said." Your two friends are fine. The lady got a little wound but she'll be all right."

An elderly man in the forefront of the bunch asked, "Can I come across?"

"You certainly can, suh."

Over his shoulder the man said a few words, uncaught by Temperly.

The man waded across the creek, the water washing around the ankles of his stout half-boots. The small bridge was further along.

Temperly let the old fellow pass. He

didn't seem to be armed.

Silvo watched them, then when Temperly moved, brought up the rear. With Temperly at his heels, the elderly cuss paused before the corpse beneath the window.

"Lenny Traylor," he said.

"Friends o' yourn?" said Silvo from behind.

The elder half-turned. "Hell, no! Used to know his maw is all."

"Your friend in the stores didn't seem to know him," said Temperly.

"Wouldn't. I knew him when he was younger. In another town. A no-good, never was anything else. Had friends with him, did he?"

"They all got their come-uppance," said Silvo.

8

"THEY all deserved their come-uppance, I guess," said the oldster. "Lenny was mindless, murderous trash and he rode with the same kind, his own stinkin' kind. Maybe they were plannin' something around here. Taking the town over or somep'n like that. But they got side-tracked here an' they got kinda drunk . . . "

"It was a good job these two gents were here," said the beanpole storekeeper. He had killed the giant called Ed and had been a mite shaky afterwards but was all right now, as was his attractive spouse.

Temperly said softly, "I guess we better tell you folks why we came to Poison Creek, though we weren't making for this place specifically when we started out, y'understand."

They were all looking at the lean man then. And the elegant woman with the white bandage on her head said, "You were welcome anyway, and I haven't thanked you enough for . . . "

"No matter," put in Temperly's partner, white hair silver in the sun from the window. "We were glad to be of service, ma'am."

Then the lean man told the three townsfolk why his *compadre* and he had passed this way, and he produced the broken derringer and asked them if any of them had seen it before.

They hadn't. They asked the inevitable questions, the main one being from the oldest person amongst them.

"Do you think that Lenny and his boys could've been responsible for that outrage back in your town, in Garrington? It sounds like their stripe."

"That'd be the easy solution to a problem," said Temperly. "And maybe even the end of a trail. But, no, we don't think now that those boys had

83

anything to do with what happened in Garrington."

"Y'see, I wondered whether you'd followed their trail to here," said the oldster.

The storekeeper put in, "Those boys came from another direction. I was at the window, I remember, and I saw 'em coming and wondered about 'em."

"Yeh, you would, I guess," said Silvo sardonically.

"If you boys have time to rest over," said the older man, "we'll show that derringer around. It's a notably fancy little thing. Somebody might remember seeing it someplace."

"We've got time," said Temperly.

★ ★ ★

Clean-up time was under way. Temperly and Silvo received congratulations from all and sundry and they, in their turn, asked questions, and Temperly showed the natty but damaged little pocket-pistol all around.

It wasn't, however, till they got to the other side of the shallow creek and into the single local saloon that they received interesting answers, which was more than they had actually hoped for anyway.

They met a local gunsmith who, they were told, spent as much time in the saloon as he did in his shop and often did business over a tot or three. And sometimes this was with a drummer friend who came to sell him goods from time to time.

"Did you buy one o'these derringers?" Temperly asked.

"No. Last time, I took me a pair o' second-hand Dragoons which I have sold since, making a mite o' profit. But I think somebody else might've bought one o' them nice leetle weapons, even the pair in fact. My colleague had a pair, y'see. The feller I mean was certainly looking mighty interested. And he could afford the price."

The man was looking about him. "Don't see him here," he added. "But

I guess he might be in later."

"What's his name and where's he at?" Temperly wanted to know.

"The feller's name is Ben Lomass and he's the son of Rancher Lomass who runs a spread called the Double Curl about five or six miles outa here."

"Is this Ben Lomass one o' them wild sons?" asked Silvo with a flash of white teeth.

The gun-seller and the oldster who had introduced him to the two pilgrims exchanged glances and the latter said, "I guess." And the gunsmith gave a little somewhat reluctant nod of the head.

"Might anybody else know whether this Ben bought a derringer or two?" asked Temperly.

"We could ask," said the oldster.

The gunsmith didn't seem as if he wanted to talk any more, as if he felt he might have said too much already.

The three others left him. They

ranged the interior of the saloon — and they asked . . .

But nobody seemed to know whether young Ben Lomass had bought a derringer or two off anybody. Everybody seemed to remember the gun salesman who was a friend of the gunsmith: they'd handled his guns and he was good. Some of them had bought guns from that source. But most folks seemed a whole lot more eager to talk about the visiting drummer — who only visited at limited intervals at that — than about Ben Lomass and his big rancher daddy . . .

"Let's go," said Temperly abruptly. The helpful oldster followed them, pointing.

★ ★ ★

As they rode, Temperly said, "We're assuming of course that the derringer was carried by somebody who was at the killing of Sheriff Oscar Brake."

"Sure," said Silvo.

"And we're assuming that the bunch — whoever — also killed and mutilated the Jolens."

"I guess," said Silvo.

"But it could be two different folk, couldn't it?"

"Two different bunches, you mean."

"Whatever."

"What you askin' me for, Temp? You're the detective, ain't you? You're the Pinkerton."

"Was! I'm a loner though, you know that. That's not to say that I ain't glad that you're along o' me right now."

"Hell's bells! You wouldn't be here at all if it wasn't for me."

"Very true," said Cal Temperly.

But the grinning Silvo wasn't looking at him, was looking ahead.

"Riders comin'," said the silver-haired man.

There were five of them, young cowboys with a guarded, wary look about them. They reined in in front of the strangers, spread out a little. They were armed but they didn't pull their guns. They looked as if they might do though. They looked fidgety, uncertain. Silvo and Temperly were two of a kind and maybe those boys recognized that.

They didn't seem to have any particular leader but one of them said, "You're on Double Curl land, gents. We're Double Curl hands. Will you state your business, please?"

Polite. Well, that was fair enough. Temperly said, "Double Curl land is where we want to be. We're looking for Rancher Lomass. Or his son Ben."

"Mr Lomass is back to the ranch-house. An' Ben ain't around right now. Anyway, we don't need no more hands."

Maybe this one wasn't very perceptive. Or he was being deliberately obtuse.

"You the ramrod or somep'n?" Temperly asked.

"No-o-oo."

"We don't need jobs. We aim to see the Lomasses on business."

The young cowhand was momentarily

nonplussed. And one of his friends said, "We could take 'em in."

"All right."

They all turned about then, became again a tightly-knit bunch. But they didn't crowd the strangers, just watched them.

The party had the spacious ranch buildings in sight when the lone rider came out towards them, riding fast as if going for a fine, fast sashay. A fine lady on a fine horse with a fine, ornate saddle. Astride, in a modish riding-habit, a pert hat, long brown hair, a handsome young face from which keen eyes peered as she reined in her horse, which snorted, was obviously raring to go.

"These gents want to see your father, Miss Berenice."

"I'll take them in. Two of you stay with me, the rest of you go on about your business." Her voice was soft, well-modulated, but it carried a firm note of authority and the boys reacted to it.

Two of them detached themselves from the main bunch, neither of them being the talky one, Temperly noticed.

The girl turned her horse about and led the way. She had appraised the two strangers but hadn't spoken to them. The three men rode behind her, the two cowboys keeping their distance.

Out of the corner of his mouth Silvo said, "This territory seems to raise some mighty fine-lookin' females."

"An' you're mighty fond of the ladies, ain't you, bucko?"

"You could say that, I guess."

The two cowboys, not having actually heard their words, looked at them suspiciously. 'Miss Berenice' rode ahead as if she were a lady officer leading a skirmishing party. She has a fine seat on that horse at that, thought Temperly — and no false modesty. He thought of the ladies that seemed to run through Silvo's life like birds at a duck-shoot.

He thought of his own lady, Tansy. He had called himself a loner, but now he realized that that wasn't strictly true

91

any more. Maybe Silvo was more of a loner.

Silvo was a hired gun. He went where he was asked to go and he liked his jobs to be simple. He hired men if he needed them, but he certainly did not, and never had, run a gang. He hadn't worked in harness with another man for any time, except Temperly, who was a friend when needed.

Temperly thought, what's in this one for me? He didn't quite know. A mystery trail. And there had been killings already. Temperly didn't try to delude himself with the thought that there wouldn't be more peril before the end, more killing probably. But he was committed now.

Again he didn't try to delude himself. He was committed to Tansy now too. But he could not return to her till this job, like many others had been, was finally finished.

9

THE ranch buildings were beautifully laid out, the spacious yard swept and still bearing marks of the wide broom that had been used. The outhouses were neat and strategically spaced for convenience and use. There wasn't a lot of litter about, as often could be seen even on the richest spreads. This had the appearance of a pretty rich one all right. Temperly had got that impression already from the attitudes of the folks back in Poison Creek.

An uneasiness. A wariness. Particularly when son Ben was mentioned. And was Rancher Lomass, monarch of all he surveyed, wanting to be monarch of Poison Creek also? That wouldn't go down at all well with the free-wheelers who revolved around that place or used it as their go-by and assignation point. Drifters! Had Rancher Lomass had problems with drifters?

So many questions. And the talky cowboy back there on the range had said that son Ben wasn't available now: words to that effect. So where was young Ben at now and had he ever owned a fancy derringer that had gotten broken?

Miss Berenice dismounted fluidly and an elderly gent came forward and took her horse. Berenice dismissed the two hands who had served chaperone, did it with two curt jerks of her head. Then she said, "This way, gentlemen," and the two visitors followed after noting that another elderly gent had come forward and was taking care of the other two horses. And the two cowboys, still mounted, were moving away quickly.

The wide verandah was as neat and well-swept as the rest of the place. It had a swinging hammock wide enough to take three or four people and a couple of well-cushioned rocking chairs.

At the side of one of these was a shining copper spittoon and that looked as if it had been industriously cleaned and polished only this morning. There was some kind of woven rush matting on the floor of the verandah and the high-heeled riding-boots of the two visitors did not clatter, just thudded.

There was a peace and an almost-silence. Out back somebody was chopping wood, but the sound was soft, almost somnolent. Strangely, in the house somewhere, somebody was playing a piano. What sounded like a Spanish piece, Mexican folk-music maybe.

Rancher Lomass had a son called Ben and a daughter called Berenice. Was the piano being played by his wife, or maybe another daughter?

Berenice led the visitors through a heavy door into a spacious hallway with a wide staircase angling from it, across this and through another door as the piano-playing became louder.

They were in a big, comfortable

sitting-room and the music came from behind a closed door at the other side of the wide expanse.

Berenice went over to this door and rapped upon it with her knuckles and called 'Father'. And the music stopped.

She had still not said more than a few words to the two visitors, had it seemed accepted them, even the strange one with the white hair who had watched her all the time, despite warning looks from his lean, dark, handsome companion.

A mighty cool girl, who turned now and said, "My father will be out presently, gentlemen."

But the first man who came through the door was certainly not her father. He was too young for that. He was dressed well; a well-britched cowhand. He had a gun at his hip and he eyed the two visitors with grey eyes from a lean, moustached face. He was bareheaded and his hair was blacker than Temperly's and longer

96

than Silvo's. A fancy Dan — but a capable one.

The two visitors were hardly aware of the girl taking her leave. Even Silvo had been distracted from watching her and instead was looking very straight at the young man who had come through the door.

"Hallo, Link," he said.

"Hallo, Silvo."

Silvo gave a little jerk of his head in the direction of his companion.

"You remember Temp, Link."

"Cal Temperly," said Link. "Yeh, I remember meeting Mr Temperly once with you."

"Hallo, Link," said Temperly. "Pleasant to see you again. But we did figure for a meet with Mistuh Lomass."

"He'll be out presently," said the lean, moustached young man. Like an echo, a few notes from the piano came through the door which Link had left a little ajar behind him.

"I'm Mr Lomass's foreman," Link

went on. "Anything you have to say to him you can say to me an' I'll do my best to help you."

"My, that's purty," said Silvo.

Link ignored him, was looking at Temperly. The latter seemed to come to a sudden decision. He reached backwards beneath his vest and he brought forth the fancy but battered derringer. As Silvo knew, his sometime partner had never been a man to waste words and could be brutally forthright.

Temperly held out the little gun and said, "We're lookin' for the owner of this."

Link's eyes widened a little but he didn't say anything right off.

And it seemed almost in mockery that he, too, reached behind him. And he brought forth what looked like the twin of the pistol in Temperly's hand. But this one looked pristine, a wicked little toy that wasn't a toy at all.

Link pointed the second derringer at Temperly who said, mildly, "Mine's not loaded."

Link smiled thinly. "Neither is mine," he said.

From behind the door a few more notes on the piano clanged. The music had been good, but this wasn't any more. It was as if whoever sat at the keyboard could hear the voices of the men outside, could hear their words even, and was reacting to them.

"This one doesn't even belong to me," Link added.

Temperly said, "We would very much like to meet the owner."

Silvo said, "We sure would."

Behind Link the door opened wide and through it came a huge old man, bent a little but with bull-like shoulders and chest, a broad, lined face and a mass of rough grey hair.

"This is Mr Lomass," Link said; then he indicated the two visitors in turn. "Mr Temperly. Mr Silvo."

Temperly had never heard his white haired friend called 'Mr Silvo' before. He didn't even know whether Silvo was his real name or not, maybe just a nickname. He sometimes called his off-and-on partner 'Silvo' but most times called him other things in a jocular manner — that was *their* way — trying to disguise, if not too successfully, his great regard for the man, a very hard man but somebody he could always rely on in the most extreme and horrendous circumstances.

Old Lomass shook hands with the visitors and eyed them shrewdly with eyes the colour of pale blue water. He had huge hands and a grip to match. It was hard to imagine those hands bringing forth the delicate notes of the Spanish tinged music that the two men had heard from behind the door.

Link reached out and took the damaged derringer from Temperly's hand. Then he held them side by side and it was very evident that they had once been an immaculate matching pair, expensive toys that could tear and kill.

Link said, "Mr Lomass, these gents

brought in Ben's other gun."

Lomass looked sternly from one to the other of the two strangers and asked, "Where did you find the derringer?"

It was the lean, dark man who answered. "Outside of a town called Garrington. Near to the body of the sheriff of that town who we think may have been killed by that gun, the killer dropping it afterwards, breakin' it an' leavin' it lie. I've taken the dead lawman's place as marshal of Garrington."

"And your name is Temperly?"

"It is."

"I have heard of you, Mr Temperly."

"People do."

"You have a wide bailiwick."

"The bailiwick, suh, of a lawman and a hunter by the courtesy of the people of Garrington — and, I might add, the murder of their sheriff, Oscar Brake, wasn't the only thing that happened there."

Lomass said, "I met Sheriff Oscar

Brake many years ago. He became well-known. I thought he had retired."

"He's retired now," said Silvo sardonically.

Lomass looked at him, said, 'Mr Silvo' — as if he was running the name caustically over his tongue.

Link said, "I have met Mr Temperly before, and Mr Silvo is an old friend."

Everybody was being excessively polite, maybe in deference to the older gentleman — but maybe not. There was an undertone of uneasiness, even of menace. And Link still held both of the derringers.

The old rancher said, "There is little use in standing here. Let's go into the study and the full story can be told." He turned and opened the door wide and led the way into the room.

It was a spacious place with wide windows and did indeed look like a man's study, a library even, with ranks of books along the high walls.

The only thing that did not fit with

the rest was the handsome mahogany grand piano that shone in the sunlight that came through the window, shone on the sheet music above the handsome black and white keyboard. It was a beautiful, lush, expensive instrument, the matching stool pushed back a little from it, obviously by the old man as he got up to go and join the three men outside the room.

There was no other door apart from the one through which they had entered the room.

Lomass moved around behind a large, cluttered desk which again looked to be made of mahogany and was of a sturdy handsomeness. He sat in a large desk-chair with arms and said, "Please take a seat, gentlemen."

The three sat on smaller, straight, rush-seated chairs in a semi-circle before him and Link placed the two guns, the pristine derringer and the damaged one, on the desk.

"I think you should tell us of everything that happened in that town,

Mr Temperly — what did you call it?"

"Garrington," said Temperly.

He launched into the narrative. His telling of it was succinct, even curt. He did not miss anything out, though, and he did not mince his words about the outrage and horror felt by the people of Garrington because of the murder and mutilation of the three members of the Jolen family.

Afterwards it was not the old man who spoke but his foreman Link, who asked, "Those Jolens, what were the first names of the mother an' father?"

It was Silvo who answered, saying flatly, "Carrie and Jim."

"Carrie and Jim Jolen," echoed Link and he and the old man exchanged glances.

"Where is your son, Mr Lomass?" said Cal Temperly flatly.

Lomass didn't reply directly, seemed to be weighing up the question. But his foreman beat him to an answer anyway. "I told you, Temperly, Ben isn't here. We don't know where he is."

Lomass looked at Link. He looked at the two other men. His eyes were like pale blue ice.

He said, "Yes, Ben has gone and we don't know where he is. He has also taken with him about a third of my herd of cattle."

There was no answer to that. And the mane-haired oldster was looking at his foreman again.

He went on, "I want you to go with Temperly and Silvo, Link, and I want you to find Ben and bring him back here, with or without the beef. And I want that crazy half-breed Digo as well."

"They're a pair of crazies," said Link. "Ben and Digo both."

Lomass didn't seem to hear his young foreman properly, or maybe didn't want to. The old man said, "I want 'em back alive."

"That's what we want," said Cal Temperly. "We want to know what they've done an' what they ain't done, if you see what I mean. I guess it's partly up to them though, isn't it?"

"Don't take too long," said the old man.

10

THEY knew the approximate direction that Ben had taken. Some of the boys had seen him with the cattle and his friend, the half-breed called Digo, as well as two other boys that they hadn't seen before. They had figured that the steers were being taken someplace else, maybe to somebody who had bought them, and that the two strange rannies were sort of collectors. They hadn't heard that that was going to happen but, after all, Ben was the boss's son.

Nobody had told them anything afterwards. The older hands were kinda peeved about that. Link placated them. They seemed to like and respect him.

He told them that he and the two men (Temperly and Silvo) were going up-country for a while on some business for the boss and that during their absence the old wrangler Dirk would be in charge.

"You mind him now."

"That cantankerous ol' goat," said one of them and everybody laughed, everybody but the two strangers who seemed to be raring to go.

"Aw, hell, Link," said one of the older men. "We'll mind him, you know that."

"Of course we will." That seemed to be the consensus.

And the trio rode on their way.

Link had other things to tell his two new partners.

But, first off, Silvo had a few cents to put in himself.

"You ranch foreman!" he said. "It sure is a far cry from when you an' me used to ride with Pal Coley an' his boys."

"Those days are finished, *amigo*," said Link. "I had the sense to realize it and I hope you have too. I always had a sneaking ambition to own a ranch."

"You don't have any ambition to

108

own the Double Curl some day, do you?" said Temperly.

"Stranger things have happened."

"Mebbe he's gonna marry the boss's daughter," Silvo quipped.

Link didn't seem put out. "Chance 'ud be a fine thing," he said.

"But Lomass has a son as well," said Temperly.

"A half-son," said Link.

"How come?"

"In confidence?"

"Sure," said Temperly and Silvo nodded his head and they both looked expectantly at the lean young man with the neat moustache.

"The old man married a young widow with one son. Ben was that son. His father was a gambler who got himself killed in a saloon brawl. Ben's about my age. We were both tads then. Ben's mother was left destitute. She was a beautiful woman though and soon had suitors. Lomass was the richest, even then. She married him.

"They had a girl, Berenice. Things

seemed to be going fine as the girl and her half-brother grew up together. Lomass an' his missus were still together when I started to work at the ranch. This is the area I came from originally, Silvo, didn't you know that?"

"Nope."

"The woman had travelled the towns with her first husband, that'd been her kind of life. And now the years were going on and her beauty wasn't gonna last forever . . . "

"Kinda poetic, ain't he?" said Silvo.

"An' his boss plays a grand pianer an' all," said Temperly.

Link ignored their sallies, went on, "It's an old story. A drummer came along, I can't even remember what he sold. He returned by night and Lomass's lady went off with him. By the time Lomass traced them, they were both dead. I guess he would've killed 'em both anyway. But they had been involved in a stagecoach disaster. The vehicle went over the edge of a cliff in a violent night gale. Everybody was killed 'cept the shotgun guard an' he'll be a cripple the rest of his life.

"Ben, who had taken the boss's name after his mom married, had always been unpredictable and nasty-tempered and the boss had got him out of lots of scrapes, including a feller almost dying after Ben knifed him. Money can talk wonders. After his mom went, Ben got even worse. He even dropped the Lomass moniker sometimes an' called himself by his real dad's name . . . And he got thick with the half-breed gunny Digo, who on'y worked for the Double Curl from time to time when we needed extra help and disappeared afterwards. And sometimes Ben with him."

Temperly said, "And were Ben and Digo missing at about the time those events we told you about took place in Garrington?"

"I think maybe they were. But they came back, and then they left again — with the cattle. Ben has allus said that a third of the herd is his by right."

The trio had found the trail of the herd but then had lost it again over a wide expanse of rocky terrain.

They still figured they were on the right trail, however. Strangely, it seemed to be taking Temperly and Silvo roughly back on the way they had come as they had made for the town of Poison Creek and then the Double Curl Ranch in the first place.

Link had other things to say and, after a pause, suddenly mouthed two names, Carrie and Jim Jolen, making both his companions jerk their heads around and look at him hard. They remembered that back at the ranch both Link and his boss had seemed to keep those names in mind.

"They had a son who was killed, huh?" said Link. "What was his name?"

"Barney," said Silvo. "He was about sixteen I guess. A pleasant kid."

Link let that hang. Then he came

up with a revelation.

"Years ago Jim Jolen worked for the Double Curl. He was a wrangler."

"He was good with horses," said Silvo.

"Carrie was at the ranch too," said Link. He gave a little spurt of humourless laughter. "She was good at other things. Not only cooking, which was why she was supposed to be there. She had an illegitimate son. That was Barney.

"Not that she wasn't good with the vittles — she was. She cooked at a dive in Poison Creek and that was where old Lomass met her. He went a bit wild after his missus left him an' then got herself killed. One night he brought young Carrie and her son Barney back to the ranch with him.

"Still and all, what happened afterwards was kind of inevitable, I guess. Carrie had eyes for other men. And one of them was Jim Jolen who was about her own age. They went off together. The old man let 'em go, seemed to anyway. I didn't hear of him trying to trace 'em . . . "

"But he could've known they were in Garrington territory, couldn't he?" said Temperly.

"I guess," said Link.

He paused. But it was obvious he had more to say, and the others waited.

"There could've been a third man of course. With Carrie, I mean. The old man; Jim Jolen; and a third. Guess who?"

"Young Ben Lomass," said Temperly.

"Looked that way. Carrying on with her at the ranch, and — who knows — mebbe he was seeing her afterwards as well."

"She was certainly a mighty accommodating female," said Silvo.

Both his companions turned and looked at him. "You too?" said Temperly.

"Yeh," said Silvo.

"You should have told me."

"Maybe I should've. I figured you'd guess, you being a sort of detective

114

an' all. Knowing you, I figured you'd tumble to it, *amigo*, I surely did."

"Maybe I have a blind spot where friends are concerned," said Temperly.

"Oh, hell," said Silvo. "I liked that woman. Older'n me. Older than her husband, I think. Jim allus seemed younger anyway. Sort of gullible. Or maybe he just didn't care. I dunno. A fascinating female, Carrie. She didn't figure she was doin' anybody any harm. It was just the way she was. No harm in her man . . . "

"Yeh, Jim was all right," said Link.

"What happened," said Silvo, "that shouldn't have happened to them. Them; and the kid on the threshold of life."

"You're breakin' my heart," said Temperly.

Silvo ignored this, it wasn't his turn to be sardonic.

"That's why I sent for you, Temp."

"I know."

"I don't know Ben Lomass," Silvo said. "I might've seen him . . . "

"Maybe Sheriff Brake saw him."

"But that doesn't mean we can pin the Jolen killings on Ben, does it?" said Link.

"You're right."

And at last they were riding on in near silence.

But they were puzzled men. And comments were passed from time to time.

Silvo: "We seem to be moving back slowly to where we came from."

Temperly: "Not exactly, I guess. We've kept to a steadier trail, easier on the horses."

Silvo: "Yeh, the riders too. And we didn't see any beef."

"We didn't see all these rocks either, all this craggy ground."

"If the beef came this way it was deliberate." This was Link. "They were driven this way to cover tracks. But I still am pretty sure they were driven this way. There've been signs."

"The light's failing," said Temperly. "Do you two want to press on?"

"You're the boss, Temp," said Silvo. He was the only person who'd ever called the man 'Temp'.

"I'll leave it to you, Cal," said Link who had stopped calling him 'Mister' long since.

"We'll press on then. I think we oughta press on for some kind of shelter anyway. See the sky ahead?"

They did. Silvo said, "Somebody might've had some o'that already."

11

THEY had had a lot of heavy rain in the Garrington territory and had had to cancel the funerals for a while. The wet had brought a certain coolness. But the bodies wouldn't last: the undertaker wanted them shifted and the preacher stood ready.

Eventually the diggers got to work. There would be four graves. One each for Carrie, Jim, and young Barney. One for Sheriff Oscar Brake.

Boot Hill was, in fact, on a hill, as it was considered all Western burial grounds should be. It was windswept and the storms had punished it mightily. Flowers were scattered, and even a few headstones likewise. The few meagre trees had already bent to the wind. In bad weather, Garrington's Boot Hill could be the most desolate place on earth.

There was mud now and the grave-men had to dig through it, squelching in their high boots, their implements clogged and slippery.

But they hit firmer stuff soon, for basically this was a dry neighbourhood. They did a good job.

The Jolens had sort of kept to themselves, only coming into town periodically for supplies. At first Jim used to drink in the local hostelry every week or so, but he never said much and didn't seem to have anybody near whom he could call a friend.

Later it seemed that he was away from home a lot. Folks saw him riding. There were tales about men who called on Carrie when Jim was away.

Now, however, the town mourned the Jolens. So cruelly murdered, brutalized.

And the town mourned the death of their favourite lawman, a mystery there, like a dark cloud.

The townsfolk followed the hearse

119

drawn by its four horses up the muddy hill, the men urging the horses on as they slipped and snorted, their forelocks splashed with mud. Because of the solemn occasion there was no muleskinner profanity now. Cajolements were almost gentle and the beasts seemed to respond to the change. Not an ostentatious equipage and the horses being just dark rather than all black, one of them with a white blaze on his nose.

Silvo, and his friend, the man called Temperly, had not returned, but Deputy Jas and his sidekick Dooley were sort of superintending things while Marshal Temperly (if he could be called that) was absent.

Some folks were pretty vocal about the new town marshal being away so long, him and his white-haired pardner not making any effort to turn up for the funerals.

Still and all, Jas and Dooley were there and so was town elder Silas Tripp, who had been mainly responsible for

120

the recruitment of gunfighter Temperly as town marshal. And, of course, most other important, or would-be important, personages were there also — with the genuine mourning family folk and kids playing hookey from school and the barflies and the whores and other kinds of rag-tag and bobtail.

And the undertaker, imposing, and almost excruciatingly cheerful. And his helper, an old twisted-up Irisher who looked like a leprechaun. And the preacher, who had a big belly, a big red face and a voice like a cracked church bell.

Somebody said to a neighbour, "I'm surprised Silvo ain't here to pay his last respects. There was almighty talk about him an' Carrie."

"Oh, hush," said the neighbour.

And the preacher's voice boomed and clanged on, awakening the echoes; and the clods began to fall dismally on the coffins and a woman wept softly. But it was soon all over, as such occasions often are, and the exodus began.

Deputy Jas was at the bottom of the hill when a horseman galloped in off the main street.

"What's eatin' you, Dale?" said Jas. "The funerals are over. You should've got here sooner."

"It ain't that, Jas," said the cowboy. "I couldn't have got here any sooner, an' I've been ridin' fast. It's just that I wanted to tell you about the Jolen place."

"What about the Jolen place?"

"All around there. Swarmin' with cattle, a whole herd. Kinda strange . . . "

Dooley was passing and he shouted, "I gotta get back to my place an' check things are runnin' all right, Jas."

Jas made his decision, shouted back, "I'm comin' your way." Said to the cowboy, "I'll go check the Jolen place."

He joined Dooley, told him quickly of the cowboy's news. The Jolen place was on the way to Dooley's little horse-ranch.

"Wants lookin' into, yeh," said Dooley. He slapped his battered Stetson with the hole in its crown on top of his sparse ginger-grey hair and added, "I didn't see any cows when I came through. I saw nothing. Let's take a looksee."

They got their horses, rode. It didn't take long. They saw the milling herd. The Jolen place looked quiet, though. It had been cleaned by the townsfolk, all horrid traces removed of what had taken place there.

"Where in hell did all that beef come from?" ejaculated Dooley.

"There are riders," added Dooley, quickly. Then Jas saw them too, four of them riding from the herd to the house. They seemed to spot Jas and Dooley and they dismounted, looking, waiting, nothing menacing in their attitudes.

But as the two mounted men got nearer the four shifted, spaced themselves out. Then, when Jas and Dooley reined in, the four were in a semi-circle around them.

Jas tweaked the rim of his hat, said, "Mornin', gents." Dooley said nothing, was looking at the four men, hard, one by one. He let his gaze come to rest on the face of the youngish man, handsome, clean-shaven, with a mane of black hair escaping from beneath his hat.

"Ben Lomass," he said.

The man's eyes narrowed and his face darkened. He didn't look so handsome then. He hooked his thumbs in his belt and took a few steps nearer to Dooley who still sat his horse. He looked up at Dooley who, like his companion beside him, had stiffened warily.

"I know you."

"Name's Dooley."

"Yeh, I remember now. You did some horsebreaking for my pa time back."

"At the Double Curl, by Poison Creek?"

"That's right. You live around here?"

"Yep." Dooley jerked a thumb in the direction of his companion. "This here is my pard, deputy of Garrington."

"Yeh, we saw he was wearing a

124

star," said one of the other men and laughed nastily. He was shorter than Ben Lomass and a whole lot darker and uglier, looked like a half-breed.

The two horsemen pretended to pay him no mind. And Jas said, "We heard there was cattle here and, as this is private property, we wondered why."

"You heard your friend, deputy," said Ben Lomass. "You know who I am." He was delving in a vest pocket. He came up with a folded paper which he handed up to Jas. "This'll tell you why me an' my boys are here with the herd. It's all straight an' above-board. We saw the place was empty. It's been left in prime condition for us. We figured the folks had already lit out."

★ ★ ★

The rain had stopped and night was falling. There were scudding clouds and no moon or stars.

The storm had been violent and even

now there was the sound of thunder in the distance and the reflection of lightning flashes.

Silvo said they could be having the storm now further on, maybe in Garrington, and that it could last all night.

"All I hope is that it doesn't come back here," said Link.

They had been caught in the open and, although they had donned their slickers, were pretty wet and bedraggled.

Silvo said, "There are some scrubby hills ahead. I guess we can find shelter of a sort there."

Temperly said, "Well, we certainly can't trail any further tonight."

The dim shapes of the hills came into view in the darkness. They didn't look much. But they had small bushy draws and the three men found the deepest of these and dug in like a trio of prairie dogs and got out their makings.

As they smoked, Silvo lit a small fire of twigs and moss under an overhanging rock in the dryness. They crouched there, taking off their outer clothing and gradually drying things, and themselves, as best they could.

They divested their horses of saddles and accessories and let them browse and they seemed well content. The storm threatened from a distance with strange rumbles and cracks but did not return.

The brush around them dried, with a dripping chorus. Silvo brewed coffee from their supplies which had been well-replenished back at the Double Curl Ranch. They sipped it gratefully. They didn't talk much. Finally they slept.

When Temperly awoke it was still dark. A black night certainly. He thought that something had startled him awake, causing him to sit up abruptly.

There was no storm though, no sound of any cacophony or violence.

He tried to get his eyes accustomed to the dark, the woolly sort of blackness.

He couldn't pierce it.

They had ground-hitched the horses. Maybe one of the beasts had gotten restless. They were quiet now: he hadn't disturbed them. But still he felt that there was something.

★ ★ ★

Deputy Jas and Dooley had wanted to see town elder Silas Tripp who, before he retired, was a fairly competent lawyer. "Twas said that he could have been a long-time judge if he hadn't when the legal pressures became a mite too much for him, gone on drunken benders, which were fairly infrequent but enough to put him 'out of court'.

Coming back from the Jolen place in the darkness Jas and Dooley very much needed the old man's advice. But, with time sometimes hanging heavily on his restless hands, Silas had begun to drink more frequently and this night it seemed had been one of the nights on which he had chosen to hoot or, as Dooley put it, go on a goddam toot.

Dooley and Jas had been shown a paper which had looked as legal as all hell. But the older man could barely scrawl his own name and Jas, who played truant from school a lot when he was a sprig, was not at all smart with the written word, 'specially if it was in any kind of legal parlance. He said big words had always given him a headache.

It was not until Jas had been taken under the wing of Oscar Brake that he had begun to mend his restless and bloody-minded ways. Oscar had given him pride, had made him a good deputy. Jas wasn't scared of man or beast — but show him a paper with long script on it and he began to go cross-eyed.

Silas Tripp was dead to the world, there was no argument about that. "We'll have to see him first thing in the mornin'," Jas had said. "More like noon," Dooley had grumbled. But there it was.

While grumbling, they'd had more than a few drinks themselves. They went to bed.

12

THE fire had died and the three men had laid themselves down in the dryness under the overhanging rock with small gaps between them in case, as Silvo had commented, one of them kicked. But they were men who had a quality of stillness about them, and a quiet wariness too.

They had taken off their gunbelts and laid them down at their sides.

When Cal Temperly had awakened he had been sure that neither of his partners had been disturbed also and now he took care not to give them alarm. He drew his gun now though, and slowly levered himself to his feet.

Peering into the strange darkness had made his eyes smart. But now he could make out the shapes of the three horses and they didn't seem to have been alarmed by anything.

One of them shifted slightly then became still. There was little sound and that died and then there was no more sound or movement and, behind Temperly, Silvo and Link slept on.

★ ★ ★

They came at him suddenly out of the melancholy night. He thought there were four of them but he couldn't be sure. Everything was too quick. On the other hand, they must have been almost as surprised as he was and thus acted hastily.

They had maybe expected to creep up on the sleeping men and take them easily. Or maybe they hadn't known that the men were there, and had merely been seeking shelter for themselves.

He had his gun, oh, yes, had taken it out of its holster before he left the bivouac. It was like a lethal appendage now. One man alone came first, a little ahead of the others. He had drawn a gun. Maybe he had had it in his hand as he moved into the rocks; maybe he had come prepared.

Even in the dark night Temperly saw the dull gleam of the weapon and he lashed out with his own Colt. He was tigerlike in his surprise, shocked by these *things. Creeping in the night.*

He felt the barrel of the gun hit hard, the impact jarring upwards to his own shoulder muscle. He felt something break beneath the steel. Then the man was down, gone.

The other came on. But now Temperly could hear movements behind him. The somebody softly called his name.

The attackers — and that they now were — had spaced out. But they seemed to be taking some sort of cover too. The light was very bad, and the night seemed too full of shifting shadows. But there was more room for a gun to be levelled now and one spoke, awakening horrendous echoes as yellow flame lanced the night.

Temperly heard somebody cry out behind him; and then he was shooting himself at the figure before him that had been briefly illuminated by the gunflash. He saw the man stumble, then turn; and the silence was like a heartbeat as the echoes died . . .

There was the scrabbling of heavy boots on rocks. The attackers were retreating.

As he went after them, Temperly almost fell over the body of the man he had savagely pistol-whipped. He could see little, only hear the diminishing sounds.

The horses were restless. He gentled them and they stayed put. Silvo joined him, said, "Link's been hit. Who were that bunch?"

"I've no idea. How bad is Link?"

"Hard to say."

"I got one of 'em. Mind you don't fall over the bastard."

Silvo gave a spurt of humourless laughter and turned, bent.

He said, "You got him good, I guess."

They returned to Link ... The lean, young, moustached foreman had dragged himself to the overhang, lay on the tufted grass of the dry ground. They could see his white face now as he looked up at them.

"Who was it?" His voice was a croak.

"We don't know," said Temperly. "But I got one of 'em and you can take a look at him later. First of all let's look at you."

"You do that," said Silvo. "I'll go back, keep watch. That bunch might try another ambush."

"All right."

Silvo went. He moved lightly. He disappeared and they didn't even hear him any more.

Temperly got down on one knee beside Link, said, "I'll have to risk some light," struck a lucifer.

Link had been hit high up in the side and was bleeding profusely. It was hard

135

to say whether the bullet was still there or not and conditions were certainly not conducive to a good examination. Temperly had tended wounds before, many was the time. He had taken bullets out. But, now, he didn't like this at all. The flickering flame went out . . .

"I want to see the man you hit," whispered the wounded ranch foreman.

"I've got to try an' stop this blood first, *amigo*. Lie still."

Link did as he had been told. His breathing wasn't good. Temperly delved in his own warbag, found a clean bandanna which he figured would have to do. He did the best he could with it. Link passed out, but his breathing got a mite better.

There were sounds of movement behind Temperly and he cautiously drew his gun. Silvo whispered, "'Pears that bunch have lit out."

Temperly pouched his gun. "Link ain't good," he said. "We'll have to take him back to the ranch. He needs

136

expert medical attention an' a bed. I've done what I can but it ain't enough."

"That bunch seemed to be goin' back in that direction, the way we came I mean," said Silvo. "Mebbe they'll try an' jump us."

"We'll have to take that chance."

"All right," said Silvo.

Link groaned. They turned to him. He hadn't been out long. He was a fighter. He said, "Cal, I want to see the one you hit."

"We'll get him."

They dragged the body back, then they both struck lucifers, made a light. Link was able to look at the bloody grimacing dead face.

"I — I know him," he said, haltingly. "But — but I disremember his name. He never worked at the ranch. But I've seen him with Ben and Digo in Poison Creek. Did you get a look at any of the others?"

Behind them a horse whinnied and another piece of horseflesh replied and there was also the sound of hooves scrabbling on rocks. "Hold it," said Silvo. He disappeared again.

He was soon back. "I found another horse."

"Must belong to this carrion," said Temperly. "Good. We'll take him back to the ranch, man and horse I mean."

"You ought to go on," whispered Link.

"Don't talk horse-shit," said Silvo.

"We'll move you," said Temperly and they both bent. "Easy. *Easy*."

When they reached the Double Curl, dawn was in the offing and folks were soon awakened. They had the body of the bushwhacker slung over the saddle of his own horse. They had had to take it easy all the way because of Link's wound. He was on his own horse but Silvo and Temperly took turns in riding beside him, holding him if he showed signs of sliding from his saddle.

The young foreman alternately rested against his horse's neck and from time to time tried to pull himself upright, but with little success. Silvo said it

138

would've been better had they had some sort of an Injun *travois*, but that was just talking into the wind, voices to reassure the badly wounded man who sometimes mumbled in return but made no words.

Rancher Lomass took charge. A fast rider was sent to Poison Creek for the doc. Lomass looked at the dead man, said he thought he had seen him before but not at the ranch. His daughter was trying to do what she could to help Link.

The dark Berenice was gentle, her eyes wide, her expression anxious. She was helped by the oldster that the two visitors had met before, name of Dirk — wrangler, ranchman, ramrod now. Lomass called him away from Link's bedside to take a look at the dead bushwhacker.

"Name was Canter," said the oldster. "He was a friend of young Ben's, Mr Lomass. And of that slimy little sidewinder Digo as well o' course."

"Link told us that," said Temperly.

"Do you know who might have been riding with him? Apart from Ben an' Digo I mean."

"He hung around in Poison Creek. Had two friends that were with him a lot." Dirk turned his head and looked at his boss. "And a boy who works here, Mr Lomass."

"That makes four," said Silvo.

"Which boy?" said Lomass.

"The one who calls himself Hideaway."

"Get him!" snapped Lomass and Dirk scuttled away.

They waited a while, drinking coffee in the cool and spacious kitchen. Dirk came back.

"Can't find Hideaway. Boys in the bunkhouse haven't seen him since yesterday evenin'. He went riding on his lonesome, maybe to Poison Creek. But he ain't come back."

With an air of decision, Temperly rose. He looked at Rancher Lomass, smiled, jerked his head in the direction of old Dirk. The dimpled scar on his face gave him a sardonic look. "Can we borrow our friend here, go into Poison Creek, make some identification mebbe?"

Before his boss could answer, Dirk said, "I can root them skunks out, I guess, an' if'n young Hideaway . . . "

Lomass interrupted. "All right. Go ahead."

Link was still holding his own but wasn't conscious. As the three men left, Rancher Lomass joined his daughter at the bedside.

On the trail to the settlement the trio passed a gig with a trotting horse going fast, another rider as escort. Yells and waves were exchanged.

"The doc," said Dirk. "Made it quick."

Poison Creek was lit up, even looked bigger now than the hole in the prairie that it actually was, the light spilling out at its edges and being reflected in the narrow strip of the water — much cleaner now than of yore — that had given the place its name.

The three men tried the main saloon

first, the only real saloon, the rest — and there were more for this was a 'wide-open' town — being dives, gambling-dens, cantinas and the like.

The young man called Hideaway wasn't to be seen, neither were either of his two pards whom Dirk said he could recognize if he spotted them.

The oldster said, "Ben Lomass and that poisonous sidekick of his, the breed called Digo, used to hang out in a hole in the wall kept by one of Digo's relatives, an uncle or somep'n."

"They might've lit out altogether," said Silvo.

"We'll see," said Dirk.

Temperly didn't say anything. Obviously the oldster had a burr in his ass about Hideaway and his friends, who were friends also of Ben Lomass and Digo. Things did sort of point to Hideaway, his being suddenly missing and all. But nothing was conclusive.

"This is it," said Dirk.

They had been leading their horses, figuring they might need them in a hurry. They hitched them at a rickety rail by an open door that spilled yellow light. There was nothing as grandiose as batwings like down at the saloon, and the window beside the door had no curtains and cracked glass so dirty that it would be impossible to see through it.

Temperly stepped forward, led the way. "If they're here just indicate 'em," he said. "Particularly if it's only this Hideaway feller and he's on his own. Questions is all so far. I want talk. I'll take 'em if I have to."

Silvo glanced at the old man at his side and said, "Do what Temp says."

"All right."

The bar was just planks of wood across scarred barrels. There were tables and chairs and not much else. The ceiling was low. A rickety fan which looked in danger of falling was revolving slowly in the low roof of the square cabin-like place and was doing little to dispel the fog of smoke.

The three men sauntered up to

the bar like weary pilgrims and, without checking with his companions, Temperly asked for rye and received a brown bottle and three shot-glasses. He glanced around him as if looking for a place to sit and said out of the corner of his mouth, "Tell me."

Dirk said, "Hideaway's in a corner near the window, seems to be on his own. Lean young feller, his hat's on the table, lotsa yeller hair."

"I see him. Maybe he just rode in for a drink like the rest of us."

"Yeh," said Silvo.

Dirk didn't say anything else.

"He's seen us," said Silvo. "Shifty-lookin' little bastard."

"Everybody's seen us," said Temperly. "Who couldn't in a small place like this? How many times you been in here, Dirk?"

"A few times. Not many."

"Yeh, well, I guess you're known. But we're strangers. Like blue-assed pigs. Everybody notices blue-assed pigs."

Dirk grinned a toothless grin and

said, "Well, that's one way of putting it." Then his eyes shifted and his expression changed for the worse.

"Them other two jaspers have just come in. Those friends o' Hideaway an' Ben an' Digo an' the others."

Temperly wanted to ask "What others?", but he thought there mightn't be time right then. And he was turning and looking straight at the door, his two companions following suit.

Silvo for one knew the signs. His old friend Temp, a fair man, was suddenly fed up of pussyfooting and was pushing for a showdown, if showdown there had to be.

The two men inside the door were both young and hard-looking and wary, their eyes darting from side to side. They must have seen the three men at the bar but gave no sign of doing this. But one of them nudged the other and they turned and went back through the door which was ajar and behind them.

Whether some sort of signal had

passed between them and the young ranny called Hideaway was something else that couldn't be determined. Whether or not, Hideaway rose quickly, walked quickly along the wall, past the window, out the door.

"C'mon," said Temperly, moving. "You stay behind Silvo, Dirk, you hear me? This might mean nothin'. It's none o'your put-in anyway."

The oldster gave a slight jerk of his head that might have meant nothing. But, as Silvo followed behind Temperly, Dirk brought up the rear. Folks parted to let them through. Eyes followed them.

At the door Temperly said, "Stay here against the wall, Dirk *amigo*. Don't come out unless you feel you ought to. If nothing happens follow us after a bit, of course."

"All right," said the old ranny now with a great air of sensibility.

Temperly flung the door wide and, half-crouching, went through with a great swiftness, turning left. He wasn't

146

seen to draw but as he looked out at the street his gun was in his hand.

Silvo followed him, turning left, and his gun was in evidence too. The two men split then, going in opposite directions. It was as if they had exchanged invisible signals.

They crossed the narrow street — little more than an alley — at a run and reached the other side where the shadows were deeper, though stray rays of yellow from the open door of the cantina dappled the walls.

There didn't seem to be anybody else around, not even a whisper of the younker with the strange moniker, Hideaway.

But the boys had been waiting. Like gooby-birds who, t'was said, are reluctant to shit in their own nests, the trio of young killers probably hadn't wanted to do anything too near to the cantina, their boozy hidey-hole.

They were Anglos and this could be called the Mex part of town and though, as friend of Digo and that

147

hardcase's relatives and friends in the favourite dive, they were welcome there, to draw attention to the rathskellar by starting a shooting-match in there or the close vicinity would be looked upon with disfavour. Mexicans could be funny folk when their quiet times were noisily interrupted . . .

A gun slashed out at Temperly from the shadows of a stinking privy but he had been holding his breath and he heard the faint sound and moved sideways and the blow only brushed his sleeve. He lashed out with his own weapon in a backhanded way . . . This was like recent history repeating itself, the night, the shadowy figures, the blow striking home.

The man went down and he lay still and Temperly turned away from him and, crouching then, tried to pierce the darkness wih his eyes. He saw nothing but the weak, fugitive bars of light. But he heard a scuffle from up where Silvo was at and he moved in that direction. There were no boardwalks on this apology for a Western street and his bootheels didn't make a lot of sound on the hard ground.

A bar of light lit Silvo's dark, grinning face, the strands of silver hair looking like wisps of flame. "I've got one here," whispered Silvo.

"I've got one back there," said Temperly.

"They weren't very good, were they?" said Silvo. "But I think one of 'em got away."

"Watch him," said Temperly. "I'll be back." He retraced his steps. When he returned he was dragging his prey, who seemed to be snoring.

There was a convenient alley. They dumped the two senseless hulks in there and lit some light. Temperly's prey was young Hideaway whose snores were turning into petulant moans. He had blood in his yellow hair and his eyes looked like the bellies of dead fish.

His pard was in a far worse state. His pard was dead, his skull split wide open by Silvo, reminding Temperly of the man he had killed in the same way not so very long ago. A heavy Colt revolver could be a lethal weapon in many more ways than one. Temperly had seen a man killed once by having an extra-long barrel of a heavy Dragoon thrust into his mouth and down his throat, not maybe as quick as the hangman's rope that the skunk had richly deserved, but just as effective . . .

13

SOMEBODY had heard something. People began to come slowly out of the cantina. The three men mounted their horses and Temperly had the now-conscious but still dazed Hideaway on the front of his saddle. One of Hideaway's friends was dead meat. The body was left where it lay.

The trio rode out, now a foursome. Nobody followed them. Now old Dirk was leading the way. He crossed the creek at a shallow place, the pebbles rattling musically under the horses' hooves. He rode a little way to the slopes of a small hill bald as a closely-shaven pate.

The night would soon be finished and the carousers returned to sleep as the morning sun rose and burgeoned. It had been a long night, a very eventful one for some people. On the other side of the creek lights began to go out.

Dirk halted his mount at a hole in the side of the hill, at its base. The mouth of a soddie. "An old prospector friend o' mine useter live here," said the veteran Double Curl hand. "Died last winter."

The cavity was bigger than it looked, sort of opened out as they crawled one by one into it, Hideaway protesting wordlessly: sort of inarticulate obscenities.

"Shut up," snarled Temperly. "Or I'll slug you again." The mercurial lean man sounded as nasty as a rattling sidewinder about to strike. Hideaway shut up, began to groan softly then, pretending greater hurt.

"Ol' Mose allus kept some tallow candles," Dirk said. He struck a lucifer, found the candles, yellow light blossomed.

There was a short blanketed bunk. "Mose was a little feller," Dirk explained, no more than a walking handful himself.

There was an upturned packing-case that had obviously served as a table, and a couple of smaller wooden boxes, one with a cushion upon it, and a backrest of the mossy wall. The cavelike place was cleaner than might have been expected and didn't smell too badly, with a mixture of earth and herb and unidentifiable odours.

"Take the best seat, bucko," said Temperly and pushed Hideaway on to the cushioned box.

The young ranny sat with his head down and his hands dangling between his knees. He was silent now. He had lost his gun back in Poison Creek. Silvo had searched him and taken a knife.

Temperly had a knife too, and he produced it now. His large, heavy-looking, wickedly sharp blade with which he was so adept. A killing blade which he pointed at Hideaway as if it were a gun.

"Look at me!"

Impelled by the rough, snarling voice the young ranny raised his head.

"You're gonna answer all my questions and you're gonna answer 'em quick. Otherwise I'll skin you alive."

"He'll do it too," said Silvo.

"Your screams wouldn't be heard in town," said Dirk. "Not from this place . . . Hell, nobody'ud take any notice anyway."

The yellow-haired boy looked apprehensive but not particularly fearful. "I don't know the answer to any of your questions, whatever they are," he said. "I don't know anything."

"You and your friends overplayed your hands back there," said Temperly. "One of you is dead an' you could be the next. And, I'm telling you, your demise could be accomplished a whole lot slower than the other feller's an' be a whole lot more painful."

"Don't he talk purty?" said Silvo.

Dirk chuckled. "He makes sense too."

Temperly didn't say anything more right then. But he moved. He moved so quickly that the other three men were taken by surprise — and Hideaway was the most surprised of all.

The knife flashed. It didn't seem to touch the seated man. But on the face a red line appeared and grew, and above it Hideaway's eyes bugged with shock.

The knife was low, a streak of blood gleaming on it in the flickering candlelight. "Just a scratch, son," said Temperly in a conversational tone of voice. "But the next one will go deeper. I can promise you that."

Hideaway's eyes dulled. "I can't tell you nothin'," he said. There was blood in his yellow hair from the earlier blow that Temperly had given him. Matted, drying. But new blood now ran sluggishly down his face and dripped off his jaw.

"Strip 'im!" said Temperly.

Silvo and Dirk advanced in the small space. The thought of his body being prepared for sacrifice seemed to scare Hideaway far more than the sting of the knife had in the first place.

"All right," he shrilled. *"All right!"*

"Just talk," said Temperly and his voice was almost gentle now. "Tell me everything you know. I'll ask questions if I think I need to."

"I was just doing what I was told," said Hideaway sullenly.

"Explain that." Temperly's voice was cutting again.

"Ben an' Digo know about you and this silver-haired man. I had a meet with Digo in the early night. He came back but not right to the ranch. He had the two other boys with him — I'd only met them once before." That could've been a lie but nobody questioned it. And Hideaway went on, "We were told to bushwhack you." The yellow-haired boy was out with all his cards now.

"You didn't do a very good job," said Temperly. "Two chances an' you bungled 'em both . . . "

"At the cantina, that was their idea. They're supposed to be professionals."

The first part of that could be another lie. But all Temperly said was, "They didn't operate like professionals."

"They surely didn't," said Silvo. "An' we'd know that."

Old Dirk chuckled. "You surely would," he echoed.

Temperly said, "Why didn't Digo come with you on this bushwhack foray?"

"He had to get back. He figured we could handle it. I had to go along with them two boys. They might've killed me . . ."

"So you're the pore innocent boy dragged into evil habits, huh?" jibed Silvo.

"The one who got away," said Temperly. "Where do you reckon he's gone?"

"He's gone to join Ben an' Digo, I guess."

"That Digo! Mebbe him an' Ben didn't care whether you got killed or not as long as you bulldogged us. Mebbe they think you know too much, bucko." Temperly's spoken cogitations seemed for a moment to go over Hideaway's head which was down

157

again, the red blood not dripping quite so badly now.

Temperly went on. "Where are Ben an' Digo at now?"

"I'm not sure. Them two boys knew. They were gonna take me up there."

"Up where?"

"I tell yuh, I don't know!"

"You sure are a pig in the middle, ain't you?" said Silvo.

"Ben took some cattle, said they were his'n by right," said Hideaway hastily. "Said he had a place to keep 'em. Wasn't gonna sell 'em over the border or anything. Was takin' 'em up country. But I swear I don't know where."

"You know Link was with us when you hit us first?" said Temperly.

"Yeh. I didn't want to harm Link. But them two boys would've killed me."

"Horse-shit," said Silvo.

"Link's shot-up purty bad," said Temperly. "We're goin' back to the ranch now an' you're comin' with us.

I ain't gonna tote you no more, you've gotta walk. It ain't far."

"I cain't walk in these boots. An' my head, it's . . ."

"You'll walk, bucko! Unless you want us to find a tree an' hang you now an' leave you to dangle like the carrion you are. Move!"

Hideaway moved. He walked and he kept on walking as the lights of Poison Creek went out behind them and the nighthawks went to bed and then dawn began to slowly break.

"Hurry, before the sun comes up," said Temperly sardonically. "We wouldn't want you to sweat. Not yet anyway."

Hideaway mumbled to himself. He hadn't the energy to raise his head and scream obscene imprecations.

He surprised them when he made a sudden attempt at a run, as if he thought he might escape. But he fell and when they soon reached him Temperly said, "Get up. Don't try that again or I'll shoot you in the leg."

But Hideaway was completely

demoralized. It was as if he had run in some kind of dream. He climbed to his feet and stumbled onwards.

When they saw the ranch it was in full daylight and the sun was beginning to rise in the distance like a ball of blood forcing itself through the morning's haze.

Riders came out to meet them and they asked how Link was faring, were told that he wasn't doing too good at all. As if this news was the last dire blow, Hideaway collapsed on his face and the boys slung him on a horse and he was toted to the bunkhouse, Dirk telling the story as they went.

Temperly said loudly, "I want him kept all in one piece for a while, mind."

"Just as you say, Cal," Dirk called back.

But Temp and Silvo couldn't tote him along after all, could they?

Besides, young Hideaway had completely talked himself out; and Dirk and his menacing pards, many of whom were erstwhile friends of Hideaway's who figured they'd been badly let down, couldn't get anything else useful out of him.

There was loud talk for a while of taking him out on the range and swinging him from the nearest tree. This didn't seem to have any effect on the dazed Hideaway, who kept falling asleep. The threats died. Although Rancher Lomass's young foreman was at death's door and maybe it had been a shot from Hideaway's gun that had brought him there, Lomass wouldn't stand for any lynch-law, that was for sure.

Everybody was worried about foreman Link, and none more than the boss and his daughter Berenice, who was close to tears when she told Temperly and Silvo the news. She looked as if she had been weeping before that.

The doc from Poison Creek would be back there again at the ranch this morning. He had done the best he could for the young man and had given him a sedative finally. And now Link was sleeping, but mumbling, not resting completely.

The two partners looked in on him again and, after exchanging glances, withdrew silently.

There was nothing more they could do here, and Temperly pondered while Silvo awaited his lead. Silvo figured he knew what Temperly needed to do. And he was right. They had to go on and try to finish the job they had started.

Berenice sat again at Link's bedside and the two partners rejoined her father for a last quick confab.

Rancher Lomass was to get in touch with the county sheriff, hand young Hideaway over to him or maybe to a couple of his representatives. Temperly and Silvo, after a fine breakfast which was now being prepared for them, were to ride on, continue with their quest. None of the three men could kid himself that that hadn't been the inevitable thing to do all along.

The fourth member of the quartet that had bushwhacked Temperly, Silvo and Link, with great hurt to the latter, was now on the loose and probably on the way to warn his friends, Ben, Digo and the rest, that their latest ploy had been only part-way successful.

Hideaway had said he only had a vague idea where Ben and the boys might be heading with the cattle. Others of the Double Curl cowboys had an idea of the direction the herd had been taken. Hideaway came up with another little nugget of information. He said Ben and Digo had been taking other beef, in dribs and drabs earlier, up country and selling it. Hideaway had sworn he didn't know where.

Temperly and Silvo had to go looking again, following a trail that had been cut in half by recent happenings — in that Ben and Digo had put a crimp in their plans and a trail that had been going warmish was now cold and the two partners felt like they might be going round in circles. But they just couldn't sit on their butts and wait for something to happen.

They were replete, re-stocked, and Rancher Lomass said, "Bring my son Ben back alive if you can."

Neither of the partners had much to say about that. Astute men, they gathered from the elderly mane-haired man's demeanour that he could figure it was hardly likely that Ben would allow himself to be taken, murderously cruel and reckless as he obviously was.

They said so-long to their new pard Dirk who, with foreman Link laid up, had to ramrod the ranch now.

In the yard the two partners met Berenice Lomass just dismounting from her horse. She was back from riding into town alone in order to pick up some new medicine the doc had fixed for Link.

More affable than usual, and not looking quite so anxious, she said she was sorry to see the two men go but quite understood why they had to leave, get on the trail again. She smiled when Silvo said that he planned to see her again if at all possible.

Riding on, the two men looked back and Berenice waved to them. And on the porch was old Dirk, and he was waving also, and Temperly said, "I kinda like that ol' cuss."

"He certainly knows how to handle himself," said Silvo. "And I hear that's he's a mighty fine cattleman too, is likely to take over permanent from Link if Link doesn't make it."

"It's a bad wound Link's got," said Temperly. "But he's a tough one."

"He's a hard one," said Silvo with conviction.

Temperly said, "The girl's gone in but Dirk's still there. We'll see 'em again, I guess."

"I aim to see that girl again, I'll tell you that, pardner!" said Silvo.

"I know your drift," said Temperly. "Yeh, but I figure Berenice is Link's girl."

"They've know each other a long time is all," said Silvo.

But it was all just chit-chat, and it died. There were grimmer things ahead and for a while they were scanning the trail and were silent with their thoughts. Temperly thought of Tansy waiting again, and as usual he didn't try to fathom Silvo's thoughts.

14

THE two boys entered the saloon in the early evening while it was still light. They were a hard-looking pair and one of them had red hair sticking out in tufts from beneath his Stetson. His companion was darker, lantern-jawed, and had a sort of milky eye. Neither of them took their hats off.

They bellied up to the bar and the redhead called for whiskey and the barman gave them a bottle and some glasses and some change.

They went to a table in a corner from where they could see both the main door and the bar and they looked about them in a sort of challenging way. Early like this, though, in the place, there were only the usual barflies and, after a cursory glance at the two strangers the usual paid them no more heed: the booze was more important.

Some of them greeted Dooley when he came in. Dooley was a likeable old cuss and he could hold his liquor with any of 'em if he felt like it. He had been helping out young Deputy Jas at the jail but, after recent upsets, things had been quieter and it looked like Dooley was about to make a night of it. When he came in this early that was usually his way.

He spotted the strangers but didn't make a point of looking at them too hard. Right off he had them pegged as a couple of drifting hardcases though and, in his capacity of temporary unpaid deputy (helping out his friend Jas anyway), he figured he'd keep a quiet swivel eye on these two.

Sometimes young hellions like that pair rode into a town and caused trouble just for the hell of it.

They were putting the booze away pretty quickly and didn't seem to be having any vittles to go with it. But maybe they had bivouacked on the trail and had a bite out there. They didn't look too dusty and neither had their horses which Dooley had spotted at the hitching-rack outside, had wondered who the beasts belonged to.

They certainly could put the stuff away — and they were talking among themselves, just the two of 'em, and they were getting loud and the redhead kept laughing, a raucous jeering of sound.

More folks were coming in now looking for a couple of quiet drinks after a hard day's work. Then some of them would be off to their wives and families, early to bed even, early to rise.

If there were any shenanigans, those usually took place after the quiet folks had gone. Most of the barflies were pretty quiet most of the time anyway, and the gambling-tables would get going and some would play and some would watch.

It was early for anybody to be doing any loud carousing. Later there might even be singing and somebody might sit at the battered piano at the end of the bar and work out a tune or two. But not yet. So the two loud young strangers were beginning to draw attention to themselves.

Still and all, thought acting-deputy Dooley, as long as they don't start any actual trouble, what the hell!

But he had a feeling deep in his gut . . .

He thought about fetching Jas . . . But hell, there were only two of 'em . . .

★ ★ ★

When the thing did happen it happened by accident — well, almost — as if the malignant fates were taking a hand and actually goading those two boys into devilry. Just in case, you might say, the booze had made them drowsy and mellow and in love with everybody, particularly the nice townspeople in this nice town.

A well-known drunk suddenly stumbled

through the batwings. He was a roaming barfly who did all the places of inebriation, always finishing up at the main saloon because his tumbledown shack was nearest to it and he could crawl home from there if he wasn't able to walk, which had been the case many a time.

He made his weaving way to the bar by devious means with folks moving out of his way and greeting him jocularly as they always did. When he was sober he was an odd-job man with squinty eyes and tangled hair who looked drunk all the time even when he wasn't. But he had good hands and could turn them to almost anything and it was hard for anybody to actually dislike him.

In his weaving progress he banged against the redheaded young stranger's chair and, as he was a heavy man with a pendulous gut, he rocked it violently, almost bringing it over and the redhead with it.

The redhead's one hand scraped the floor and he managed to right himself, lever himself upwards. But his chair went over with a clatter. The cacophony startled everybody. Heads turned.

The redhead turned and hit the staggering drunk in the mouth, flooring him. The drunk carried the obligatory hip pistol but nobody could remember ever seeing him use it. He had been jostled by many and seldom took umbrage. Maybe it was just because he objected to being jostled by a stranger — hit in the mouth, by cracky, and blood already trickling down his chin — that he foolishly went for his gun now.

After his swing the redhead was still a mite off-balance but even so, the drunk couldn't possibly have beaten him. But then: "Hold it!" a voice rapped. It was Deputy Dooley and he had been watching the two strangers closely and, right at the start of the trouble, had drawn his gun. And now he levelled it.

The redhead, his own weapon only

half-drawn, let it slide back into its holster. The oldster was scrawny, but he looked mighty determined.

The redhead's dark milky-eyed friend had been left out of the action and was peeved about that.

He also couldn't stand his booze like his partner could and it impaired his judgement more than somewhat.

He drew his gun. And Dooley shot him.

The slug bored into his shoulder, throwing him backwards. Then in a sort of reflex action he came forward across the table and his gun hit the top and skidded among spilled liquor and broken glass and finally thudded to the boards.

More guns were being drawn and horrendous hell could have broken forth. And, in the middle of this fraught scene, the drunk who'd been the catalyst to start it all, stood, bloody mouth agape.

The redhead grabbed him, stuck a gun in his back and yelled, "No more!

Or he gets it." Over his shoulder he said to his wounded pard, "Move, go on!"

Clutching his shoulder, blood bursting through his clawed fingers, the dark young stranger with the one milky eye turned awkwardly and staggered for the door, his desperate momentum carrying him through the batwings.

They got to their horses and mounted up, the redhead still holding the squirming drunk who was squealing now like a pig being led to slaughter. The redhead pistol-whipped him and he fell in a heap. The two men forked their horses and set them at a gallop, the wounded younker holding on grimly.

By the time Dooley and the others got out on the stoop the two riders were at the end of the street, had turned around the bend of the houses and were out of sight, the sound of the galloping hooves quickly fading.

Deputy Jas came running down the street and his elderly partner Dooley tripped to meet him.

"Who got shot?"

"A stranger." Dooley quickly told Jas what had happened.

He pointed, went on, "They're going in the direction of the Jolen place, seems like. Two of 'em. Hardcases. I've got a feeling . . . "

"You think they might be part of that new bunch?"

"Ben Lomass an' the others who've taken over that place? Yeh, that's what I'm thinking."

Jas made a quick decision. He said, "I'd surely like to look at that place again, that bunch. But not just you an' me this time, pardner. We'll take a posse."

"There'll be volunteers all right," said Dooley firmly, half-turning to look at the pistol-whipped drunk who was being hauled to his feet by willing hands. The man's face streamed with blood and he looked bemused, pitifully beaten.

"Yes, we've got an excuse to take a posse out all right," said Jas. "You

175

get a bunch together, pardner, as many as are willin' an' capable. I'll get the horses and my rifle. I'll bring your long gun."

Volunteers were indeed numerous and vociferous, among them many of the wounded drunk's barfly cronies who had to be dissuaded from getting their cayuses and joining the party. Most of them could fall off before they reached anyplace important, but Dooley didn't put it to them in that way. The cantankerous oldster could be a soul of diplomacy when he needed to be.

He told the boys to look after their friend and they surrounded him and guided him back through the batwings, the doc, who had been quickly summoned, bringing up the rear. Doc was always good for a few free drinks anyway.

A bunch of mounted and well-armed men rode out of Garrington. Ben Lomass, if up to no good, could have more men now (the redhead and his wounded pard could be two of those, of course), but the posse was adequate, Deputy Jas figured, and mighty determined.

They remembered the Jolens, so recently put under the sod. And they remembered Sheriff Oscar Brake likewise. The terrible questions still clustered in the air like malignant bats and, who knew, some of them might be answered this day. The Jolen place was the catalyst and maybe the solution to the mysteries — where it had all started — lay there after all.

15

THE wounded man had fallen from his horse and was on his knees before Ben Lomass with Digo at his side and most of the other boys grouped around. Ben had gotten in other gunnies and the redhead, who still bestrode his horse, and his shoulder-plugged friend, were two of them.

Saturnine Ben with his mane of black hair had an evil look in his dark eyes.

"Godammit," he said, his voice deep with emotion. "I told you! I said nobody was to go near that town unless I said so. And there might be a posse on your heels at that. Is there?"

"I don't know," said the redhead. He was still all in one piece but his wild ride on the hooch he had imbibed had given him a roaring headache. He was a mean cuss who was good with a gun.

Ben had bought his gun-hand, but hadn't actually paid for it yet, and now the redhead figured he didn't like Ben's manner, didn't like it one little bit.

Hell, him and his pard had only been getting a quiet drink for themselves and looking at a fresh town for future reference. That they had tried out trouble as well didn't enter into his thoughts now.

"To hell with it," he said. "Get Billy fixed up an' we'll be on our way. Thanks for the work, Ben, though we ain't done nothin' yet. But I guess we'll pass now anyway."

Beside Ben, pard Digo stood there like a dark poison-toad, bent a little as if he were about to start jumping. He didn't take his black raisin eyes off the redhead.

"Get Billy fixed up," sneered Ben Lomass. "Hell, he's no good to us any more an' it's his own fault, and yours. I'm gonna shoot him."

The wounded man gave a loud cry and lurched to his feet. He clawed for his gun but it wasn't there, had been left in the saloon back in Garrington.

Digo's attention was momentarily diverted as he drew his gun, his partner Ben doing the same. But the redhead was drawing too, and even as his wounded pard was driven back to the sod with a bullet in the temple from Ben's gun, the redhead was levelling his.

Other men were moving too, though with no pre-ordained purpose it seemed. The men, gunfighters all, reacted, and the redhead's horse reared in the middle of it.

Digo and the redhead exchanged shots and they missed each other. But Digo's slug didn't miss the redhead's horse: it scored a thin red line across his neck and he squealed and turned and bolted, taking his rider with him; and they went like the wind.

"Stop him," screamed Ben Lomass. "He knows too much."

Shots were flung after the runaways but with no success, and they were soon out of range. Men scrambled for their horses.

★ ★ ★

The posse was almost in sight of the Jolen place when they saw the fleeing horseman who came nearer before veering off.

"It's that redhead," yelled Dooley. "He's on his own."

"Get him," said Deputy Jas.

The fleeing horse was panicked, erratic, his eyes rolling. He suddenly went off in a direction his rider hadn't chosen for him and no amount of cursing and pulling at the reins would change him. The posse surrounded horse and rider.

"They shot my pard," said the redhead, his hands in the air in surrender. "And they're after me."

Jas had to think quickly again, and he was getting good at that. He said,

"Two of you stay with him, take him in that outcrop over there." He pointed at a cluster of boulders big enough to shelter horses and riders. "Tie his hands. You, Tally, Mickle, jump to it."

Tally was a hard-bitten oldster, Mickle little more than a boy, but a tough and intelligent one. They were the blacksmith and his assistant and they always worked together fine, as they did now, no argument, no words at all except to the prisoner as they divested him of his gear, hard-rock Tally growling, "Move your ass, pilgrim."

"I ain't arguin'," said the redhead, grinning. "I'm all tuckered out." Then he shot over his shoulder, "Watch that bunch, my friends, they ain't up to any good and they ain't amateurs either."

"Here they come," said one of the posse-men.

"Dismount an' get down behind that rise over there," ordered Jas. "Hold your horses, don't let 'em go."

It was the time when the days were long, the evenings light. But the light was failing now and soon the night would fall with a suddenness like a dark blanket.

★ ★ ★

"We're going back towards Garrington," said Silvo.

"So we are," said Temperly. "But we've been followin' the signs all the way, haven't we?"

"Such signs as there were," said Silvo. "An' precious few. I hope we've been followin' the right signs."

"You know this territory better'n I do. Where exactly are we now?"

"Exactly ain't possible, particularly now the light is going. But I figure if we go in a straight line we'll be goin' somewhere near the Jolen place."

They rode on in silence, with Silvo a little in the lead then.

The sound of gunfire was carried to them on the breeze in the still greyness.

"Trouble," said Temperly, almost as if he welcomed the sound. He spurred his horse past Silvo who, however, soon caught up with him and they rode hard.

The shooting seemed to come from the other side of an outcrop of boulders that suddenly loomed up before them. Three men appeared on horseback and Temperly and Silvo reined in.

There was the glint of steel and for a moment things were mighty fraught. Then Silvo said, "Tally."

The figure was big and substantial even in the half-light. Tally, the Garrington blacksmith, and, a little behind him, his youthful assistant Mickle, who seemed to be watching a third man, afoot, somebody neither Silvo or Temperley recognized.

"Silvo," said Tally. He didn't know Temperly very well. He went on, "A mob have taken over the Jolen place. Two of 'em started trouble in town. One's dead. This is the other one." He jerked a huge thumb in the direction of the unarmed stranger who didn't seem as if he was bothered much about anything right now. "We got him. But the rest attacked the posse which was brought out by Jas an' Dooley. Jas told me an' Mickle to watch this jasper. He might be able to tell us a whole lotta things."

"Stay there," said Temperly, glancing then at Silvo, adding, "C'mon, *amigo*."

"I'm with you," said the silver-haired man peevishly.

"Wait," said Tally, and he could be as peremptory as acting-marshal Temperly. "You don't want to get shot at by your own people. Go with 'em, pup. I'll look after this jasper."

Young Mickle rode forward, led the way. They rode close to the saddle, their heads down. And then Mickle called out and all three of them dismounted from their horses and led them on.

The shooting was spasmodic, Jas's defending party crouched down below a rise, the attackers sort of wheeling

185

about still mounted, not so well covered. Deputy Jas, who spoke to the newcomers now, had chosen his spot well. There were no casualties yet; they didn't know about the other side.

The two parties were pretty evenly matched, with maybe the law party, with two new volunteers — three with young Mickle — having an edge now.

Bullets zipped over the men's heads; and the darkness was here. It was lit by lances of yellow flame and the gunshots crackled and rolled and sent back ghostly echoes. As yet there didn't seem to be any moon or stars, just scudding clouds. The men were firing blind now, but the attackers, mounted as they were and with no cover, lit by the garish flashes, were momentary targets like spectres appearing and disappearing.

A man cried out in mortal agony and, suddenly, the attackers were in retreat. Deputy Jasper turned towards Temperly, effectively handing over command to him.

Temperly shouted, "They'll be takin' cover at the ranch. Mount up. Let's get after them."

They rode past a prone figure in the grass. A riderless horse galloped in front of them and, ahead of him, the Lomass and Digo bunch pushed their horses as the dim bulk of the erstwhile Jolen dwelling began to show.

Suddenly both bunches of riders were among milling cattle, a herd that seemed to materialize out of the night. Progress was slower. Shooting had stopped.

The first bunch of riders made it to their destination, and now they had the cover, the advantage. The only shields the posse had were the cows.

With a wave of his hand, Temperly halted his men. "Drive 'em back," he yelled. "Bunch 'em together."

Silvo, Jas and Dooley, who were nearest, got the idea of what he planned to do — and they passed it on. Bullets were raining from the house. A man cursed loudly as a slug took his hat off and it disappeared among the herd. A retreat was in order. But it had a double purpose.

16

IT was a bigger herd than it had at first seemed. As Temperly and Silvo knew, it was a third of the Lomass Double Curl, with maybe some earlier extras added to it, gathered piecemeal by Ben and his minions.

As the posse pushed the first bunch back, and out of firing range in fact, they gathered more. Steers are gregarious creatures, and they came forward from all directions, lowing in their mournful way but as happy as cows can be in the company of their own kind and a few seemingly friendly humans to boot.

Soon the men were bunched together too, at the back of the herd. Dooley, who had acted as scout, came back. "We've got 'em pointed dead right," he said.

"Drive 'em," said Cal Temperly and

he drew his gun and fired it into the air.

Others did the same, but not wasting bullets. And they screamed and *yippied* as the herd began to move in a sluggish mass.

But they gathered speed quickly and the thudding of their passage was like a myriad drums.

They hit the Jolen place head-on, with the main spearhead right at the main building, steers pushing, their companions behind almost climbing on their backs. And, if anybody was shooting inside the building, there was no sound of that, and even the swaying boards and logs could not be heard as they rumbled, cracked and splintered — there was only the horrendous sound of the herd.

The walls gave and the whole front of the house collapsed inwards and the steers were scrambling and falling over each other and pushing and roaring in the dust and the flying timbers.

The herd went right through, taking

most of the house with them. The posse, following, found the human bodies among the debris.

They dismounted. They were still cautious, carrying a gun in one hand while they did other things with the free hand that remained.

"Some of 'em got away," yelled somebody.

"This one didn't," said somebody else, standing over a still body, its throat crushed by a shard of timber, the face miraculously untouched but horrific in its expression: staring eyes, bared teeth.

A man was groaning monotonously. They found him crouched in a corner, the only corner that was left in the shambles of the twisted wreckage. He was protected by a small section of splintered logs and there was a section of roof over his head but this already creaked alarmingly as two men approached it.

The wounded outlaw screamed as they dragged him quickly out of harm's way and, as if on a signal, the corner collapsed upon itself in a shower of dust.

"He's dead," said Silvo. The man's cry of protest had been his last.

"Here's another one," said a posse member, and then Dooley was by his side.

The oldster bent. "It's Ben Lomass," he said. "What's left of him."

Silvo and Temperly joined Dooley. Temperly said, "He ain't gonna be any more trouble to his family, or to anybody else."

"Yeh, he got his come-uppance all right," said Dooley.

Ben's mane of thick hair was a strange colour now, so matted was it with blood. All one side of his face was caved in and his head was at an odd angle, thus the blood had run in strange directions: there wasn't much of it on his tattered clothes. His legs were pinned by a wide shard of timber, obviously a part of the apex of the roof. There were indications that he had tried desperately to free himself before his head had been trampled in and his life extinguished. He was no longer a handsome and wicked boy but a pitiful thing.

The posse went right through, ranged outside. "Looks like the rest of 'em found horses an' got away," said Deputy Jas.

"And Digo among 'em, I guess," said Silvo. "And that's a shame and a goddam facer."

"Digo?" said Jas. "Is that that poisonous-lookin' little half-breed?"

"It is. I'm hopin' he got tromped an' will die on the trail."

"We've got to find out about that all right," said Temperly. "That snake mustn't be left alive. It seems to me that he might be worse than Ben Lomass ever was."

"I think I know what you mean," said Silvo.

"I want to talk to that prisoner who was left with the big feller," said Temperly.

193

"Tally, you mean. He'll be there, prisoner an' all. I hope ol' Tally ain't had to bust his head. There's young Mickle."

They followed the youngster to his boss who was sitting in the midst of the cluster of boulders with a gun in his hand. The prisoner, a tough-looking young redhead with a quizzical expression, was sitting opposite the huge blacksmith. They were both smoking.

"You're the lucky one," Temperly told the redhead. He stretched a point. "Most of your friends have been crushed to death."

"Dead or alive, they ain't no friends o' mine," said the redhead.

The moon was out now and there was more light. The redhead squinted up at the lean man who stood above him. "You're Cal Temperly," he said. "You used to be a Pinkerton. I saw you once capture a man down on the Brazos."

He pointed in the direction of what

was left of what had once been the Jolen abode. "I'll tell you all I know about Ben an' Digo an' the rest of that bunch, Mr Temperly."

"Ben's dead," said Temperly. "But we think Digo is still on the loose, so we haven't got much time. Talk fast."

"Ben shot my wounded partner," said the redhead. "I vowed to myself I'd get Ben, but I don't have to do that now, do I?"

"No. Go on. *Pronto.*"

"Digo's the worst though. Ben was crazy. Digo is crazier. He likes hurtin' folk in the worst possible ways. He likes torture an' killin' . . . "

"It figures. Go on."

The redhead told what he knew to the impatient Temperly while the others stood by. It was not a pleasant story.

★ ★ ★

Ben was dead and Digo was alone. The other boys had split off from

195

him. He hadn't seen them go. He was known in this territory now and the posse would be after him. The other boys weren't known. They were probably making for the border, would lay low for a while over there. The rich pickings they had been promised by new rancher Ben Lomass would never materialize now. But there were other places, other jobs.

Digo didn't know what was in store for him. He was wounded. He figured that if he didn't get help soon he would maybe die.

He was suffering. He had made many other people suffer, then he had killed them. He didn't want anything like that to happen to him. He was like a sick coyote seeking shelter — and more.

He had a bullet in his side, high up, in among his ribs, he thought, deep. He certainly wouldn't have been able to get at it. Maybe nobody could. He hadn't had time to do much.

The cattle stampede had been

something totally unexpected. Those people from Garrington had acted like devils. Their devilish trick had made Digo scream with crazy laughter — before he yelled at his *compadre*, his devil's pardner, to come, to make a run for it. But then he had seen Ben fall, become pinned, crushed, his eyes bulging in death.

Digo would have tried to save him. Ben was the only person in the world he would've tried to save. But it was too late. Ben wasn't Ben any more: he was just a dead carcase and Digo had seen many like that.

He was turning away from the carcase when he was hit. He had not heard the shot over the rampaging roar of the frenzied cattle but he had felt the slug going into him, just a slight blow at first, and then like a red-hot poker.

The pain got worse as he staggered through the debris, the world falling about him. But he had found his horse, managed to climb on the beast's back, and he had rode. He knew others had escaped and were riding; but not Ben, *not* Ben.

After a bit, and there didn't seem yet to be any pursuit, he had slowed down. He could feel the blood flowing from him, into his pants, down over his saddle. He was a small man. He didn't know he had so much blood. He shouldn't lose so much blood!

He fumbled, cursing weakly, obscenely; he fumbled in his warbag and found a bandanna and wadded it and pressed it to his side, his fingers quickly becoming dappled with warm blood which soon became sticky.

He took off his thin snakeskin belt, knowing that his gunbelt would hold his pants up if he ever got out of the saddle: he felt he might fall out . . .

He managed to strap the cloth to his side but he knew it wouldn't hold very well, or for so long. The bandanna, the thin belt, the whole protection — and it was meagre — was becoming sodden with blood. He felt that his life was draining from him . . .

The pain seemed to get less and it was as if he was riding through a fog, no night, no moon, no stars. He knew this was not good.

He managed to haul himself upwards and out of it and then the pain attacked him again with a burning fury. He felt he was falling and he grabbed his saddle and held on grimly. Then he saw the lights of the town.

He had been letting his mount take the lead and the beast had had horse-sense. The beast was heading for rest and warmth and sustenance. But what of his rider?

"Madre de Dios!" cried Digo. He was paying for his terrible sins.

17

THE main street was empty. The lights were few and Digo was surprised that he should have seen them at all. He couldn't see very well now. The fog was coming back.

There was no sound except the clop-clop of the hooves of Digo's horse. The beast was in no hurry now. He could smell water but he wasn't aiming to gallop for it.

The horse-trough was outside the saloon and the saloon was in darkness and the moonlight didn't shine on this side of the street.

The horse nosed forward to the trough and dipped his head gracefully and drank.

"Damn you," said Digo. "Go on. *Go on*."

He used his spurs and they were brutal Mexican ones, but the horse took no notice. He could tell the man was weak. He was not a good man and had no respect for horseflesh. He was a cruel man.

His rider leaned across the beast's neck. He was a lightweight man but the horse could feel the dead heaviness of him now and ignored it and went on drinking.

Digo straightened himself a little and the pain tore at him like red-hot and cruelly sharpened knives. He tried to pierce with his eyes the veil of fog that seemed to be all around. But its density fluctuated now, coming and going with the waves of pain that were like a goad. And Digo saw something! His eyes were, in fact, drawn to that something by the sound it made, a metallic creaking as the soft wind blew it gently to and fro.

"Move," Digo said, and he used his spurs again. The horse had drunk his fill now, and he moved. He ambled. That's a doctor's shingle, Digo thought, up there creaking in the wind. He halted the horse, and the beast stood docilely.

There was a short flight of steps up to a small porch. Digo fixed his eyes on those steps, which seemed to be wavering. He climbed down painfully out of the saddle, and he felt the blood running from him. He lurched across the narrow boardwalk and reached the steps and went to his knees.

He was not able to raise himself and he went up the steps on his knees. He reached the porch, the door. The small sign creaked above his head as he held on to the post at one side of the porch and hauled himself upwards. He groaned. He couldn't raise his head.

He took out his gun which was sticky with blood. He reversed it and hammered on the door with the serrated butt with the knife-cuts upon it. He had started once to notch it for every man he had killed, that he claimed he had killed fairly, for he was good with a gun.

He had stopped counting, stopped

cutting. The sweat-stained serrated butt of the Peacemaker Colt .45 fitted snugly into his hand, comforting him. The Peacemaker. Digo felt like laughing. Hell, he was no peacemaker, never had been. And he told himself now that he wasn't about to run his string yet. No!

There was the sound of footsteps behind the door and a querulous voice shouted, "All right, I'm coming."

A bolt was drawn, a key turned in a lock. As the door was opened, Digo reversed the Colt again and pointed the muzzle forward.

A figure stood before him in a dressing-gown. Stooped, peering, elderly obviously but not very plain to Digo.

"I'm hurt, doc," said Digo. "Let me in."

"I'm no doctor." The querulous voice was mighty snappy now. "And you don't need that gun anyway."

"Your shingle's up there."

"That's a lawyer's shingle. I'm a lawyer. Used to be anyway. You're not

203

seeing very good, are you, friend?"

"I need help. I want a doctor."

"So I see." The querulous voice had softened a little. "Put your gun away and come inside. I'll do what I can for you. I'll get you a doctor."

★ ★ ★

Silas Tripp's lawyering had brought him plenty of prestige in the community of Garrington. He had done a short spell of judgeship also but, because of his fondness for strong drink after his wife died childless, had found the solemnity of presiding over court session a little too much for him, a view shared by his 'betters' in the profession. Silas's spasms of levity on the bench were too numerous and, although such spasms endeared him to a great number of the venal public, they were considered too outspoken and ribald for his profession, bringing it into disrepute.

Silas was mighty easy about it all. He was much happier helping his friends and neighbours (and now and then a congenial visitor) with their problems than sitting on an august bench and pretending to be stern with barflies and brawlers when he didn't feel stern at all. But he had a short way with scum and was short also with whippersnapper lawyers who defended such scum. He was outspoken and of times insulting, and that didn't go down well with his mealy-mouthed contemporaries at all.

This is scum, he thought that night, knowing who his wounded visitor was. Silas was a well-respected elder of the town. The townsfolk had never judged him as he had been expected to judge many of them. He still had power, which he used gently. He had made Cal Temperly town marshal, and Temperly wanted this man, this spiderlike scumhound with the gun — who would not sheath the gun now.

Silas said, "I'll take you to a doctor. I'll take you the back way. People will be getting up now. There won't be so much chance of us being spotted out there though. I don't want anybody to get hurt."

"You lead the way, old man," said Digo, his voice thick.

"I can't go out like this, that'd maybe draw attention to us."

"Put somep'n else on then. Hurry up!" Digo sat down heavily on a well-stuffed armchair.

Silas hoped the man wouldn't be able to get up again. But Digo rested his elbow on the arm of the chair to steady it and kept the gun pointing at the older man. His wound was in the other side, the left, and the blood was evident in the growing early-morning light.

"I ought to try an' fix something on that bad place," said Silas. "You're losing too much blood."

"I know it. Don't try an' trick me, ol' man, or I'll shoot you an' go find the doc myself."

The dark spiderlike man was keeping himself upright in the chair through sheer cussedness. "My pants are upstairs," Silas said.

"That does it," said Digo. "You're a cunning ol' bastard, ain't you? I ain't lettin' you outa my sight. Move. Just like you are. Anybody gets in our way will get shot, I promise. And you with them. Move, I said!"

Silas moved. And Digo made it out of the chair. The human body could stand a lot and the crazy little half-breed was pushing his to the limit, torn and battered as it was. As he followed Silas he left a trail of small bloodspots on the worn carpet.

Silas led the way along the backs of town, among the privies and rubbish piles and odd lumber ethereal in the half-light, misty from the haze coming off the prairie.

Silas nimbly skirted a rusty old broken ploughshare. Digo was startled by the manoeuvre. Maybe, in his condition, he hadn't even noticed the obstacle, which the older man had spotted, used.

Digo tried to match Silas's swerve — and didn't quite make it.

He caught his ankle on a protruding piece of jagged, rusty metal and he staggered. And Silas turned on him with a swiftness that was totally unexpected. But Digo was a wild one, as cunning as any animal — or any old lawyer — and, even as he fought to right himself, he lashed out with the gun.

The steel barrel caught Silas a glancing blow on the temple.

He felt it, heard it as a sort of *clang* in his brain. He felt himself falling and the world went darker around him.

He fell on his back and looked upwards at the dim, half-crouching figure, saw the glint of the gun barrel pointed straight at him . . .

★ ★ ★

They saw the horse first, lying on its side, still alive but obviously in great pain. Then they saw the man. He was clambering to his feet. As he stood upright he raised his hands above his head. He peered.

"I cain't go any further," he said. "That you, Red?"

"It is, Randy," said the redheaded captive.

"They got you then?"

"They got me all right, pardner."

"Who's this?" said Cal Temperly.

"Just one o' the boys, one o' Ben's suckers, like me. Joined up 'bout the same time me an' my pardner did. We knew him from way back."

"My hoss's leg's broken," said Randy plaintively.

"Shoot him," said Temperly. "Put him out of his miscry."

Suddenly the posse bristled with drawn guns. Randy, who was scrawny but fast-looking, with a yellow cowlick, looked a mite uncertain, drew his gun slowly. He didn't look at the rest of them as he walked to his fallen horse and shot the beast through the head.

The echoes died. The captive Red, who had talked so well, spoke up.

"You don't need us any more, Mr Temperly, me an' Randy."

"He's right, Temp," said the silver-haired man at the side of his lean pardner with the crooked scar.

"Let 'em go, Temp," Silvo added softly. "They're just gunnies who were hired for a job."

Temperly knew what his old partner was implying. He was implying that he and 'Temp' were little more than paid gunnies themselves. And maybe he was right.

Temperly looked at the boy called Randy, asked, "Have you seen Digo?"

"Yeh, but not to speak to. I think he'd been wounded. He was making for that town."

"I didn't figure that," said Temperly softly.

He raised his voice. "All right, you boys can go, but you'll have to use the one horse."

"We'll use my horse," Red said.

"Yeh," said Randy eagerly. "*Yeh*."

"You keep away from that town!"

"We will, o' course," said Red. "We'll make for the border, won't we, Randy?"

"Sure."

"Get going then," said Temperly.

Randy mounted up behind Red. The posse watched them go. The light was getting better.

They hit the town and they heard the two shots on the still air. "Round back," yelled Dooley, who hadn't said a word for miles. Deputy Jas said nothing but urged his horse forward, wheeled him towards the nearest alley.

Temperly turned to Silvo, to Dooley, ordered, "Stay this side, there might be others hidin'." He didn't wait for an answer, even a nod; he wheeled his horse after Jas.

They saw the man on the ground and, turning in his saddle, Jas yelled, "It's old Silas Tripp."

"Look after him then."

They both dismounted. There was nobody else in sight.

Suddenly a man in shirt-sleeves leaned

from a door, peering inquisitively. And there were windows open, shadowy figures beyond them.

A shot was fired from the shelter of a privy and the bullet winged its spiteful way between Temperly and Jas. The latter flung himself forward and down. He crouched beside the prone form of the old lawyer. The man in shirt-sleeves drew himself quickly out of sight. An upstairs window creaked, but there was no menace there.

Temperly lay flat behind a hump of ground, a pile of dried rubbish actually, which stank like a dying skunk. He stared at the privy ahead of him but could see no movement there.

The leaning door which looked as if it had been petulantly kicked, and whittled on also maybe, was slightly ajar. But Temperly knew the shot hadn't come from in there. It had come from *behind* the leaning, wooden, battered structure where the cover was better, two thicknesses of timber and what was in between.

The next shot made a booming, echoing sound. The bullet went past the crouching man's elbow. He flung himself sideways and rolled. He came to rest on his side and he fired three rapid shots at the privy.

There were two answering shots but it seemed that the man in cover had miscalculated. The slugs spat up the dirt between Temperly and the rubbish lump behind which he had been lately crouching.

He rose and ran, half-crouching, and as he did so a strange sound assailed his ears.

He would have been hard put to describe it. He might have said that it sounded like the braying of a dying mule. Or a dying laughing hyena — although he had never seen or heard a laughing hyena. He had heard a mule dying once and making a sound like that after having its throat torn out by a mountain cat.

He ran to the side of the privy. And around it.

Digo lay on his back. His gun was at his side, thin wisps of smoke still drifting from its muzzle. His arms were stretched out above his head, his hands open and the fingers spread as if he had been crucified against the hard earth.

He looked up at Temperly and he said, the words burbling, the laughter behind them in the throat, "You didn't kill me, you smilin' son-of-a-bitch, I was dead already."

And he was still making that hideous mocking sound till, quickly and suddenly, he did finally die, though he still stared up at Temperly, the black shoe-button eyes set in hate.

The lean man left him there and went back across the hard, littered ground. Silas Tripp was sitting up, Deputy Jas's arm around his shoulder.

The old man said, "He was badly wounded, wanted me to take him to the doc. I jumped him and he slugged me. Then he tried to shoot me, twice, and he missed both times. He wasn't seeing very good."

"No," said Temperly.

He felt the tension drain from him: it was like an anticlimax.

Silvo and Dooley appeared and the latter said, "The town's clean."

Temperly said, "Digo's over there behind that privy." He pointed. "Drag him out."

"The shithouse," said Silvo and he chuckled evilly, added, "That's very appropriate, don't you think?" Nobody answered him. Folks were coming out of their back doors.

Epilogue

"IT'S all true what Temp's told you, Mr Lomass," said Silvo. "I'd swear on a bible to that."

The lean man with a puckered scar on his face gave his partner a sidelong glance. The thought of the silver-haired and notably amoral gunfighter swearing on anything was more than slightly ludicrous.

Dooley got into the act too, saying, "It's right, I'd swear to that too."

There was just the three of them at the Double Curl Ranch, seated in a semi-circle around the huge desk with the big mane-haired elderly man perched on the other side of it.

Lomass said, "I believe you. Why wouldn't I?" His voice was deep, soft, sad. He went on: "So Ben was killed by the very herd that he took away with him?"

"Nothing more nor less," said Temperly.

Dooley said, "I'd like to visit the bunkhouse, Mr Lomass. My two friends will tell you the rest of it. They know more about all the ins and outs than I do."

"All right," said the rancher and Dooley turned to leave. He was known pretty well at the Double Curl, having sold horses there. He was an old friend of the equally elderly Dirk, acting-ramrod at the ranch now, he who had been so good in helping out Silvo and Temperly during the Hideaway episode. That young hardcase was already in the charge of two of the county sheriff's deputies.

Another deputy, known to all and sundry as 'Jas', was back watching over the now quiet town of Garrington, had allowed his own acting deputy Dooley to take the trip to Poison Creek and the Double Curl spread with Silvo and Temperly.

Rancher Lomass said now, "How

about Digo?" The inevitable question.

"He's dead too," said Temperly flatly. "He was worse than Ben. Far worse."

That was debatable. There was no remark from the man behind the desk, and the speaker went on. "Digo tortured the Jolen family, made Jim Jolen sign a paper handing over the spread to Ben, a bill of sale you might say. Then Jim, Carrie and the boy were killed. Jim Jolen, after he left here with Carrie, had an arrangement with Ben. Before he went the whole hog an' took a third of your herd, Ben was picking at the stock and taking it up country an' selling it to Jolen. I guess there was still a thing going with Ben and Carrie also . . . "

Temperly's voice faded. But Rancher Lomass had nothing to say — and neither had Silvo. And the lean talker told the rest of it in his deep, well-modulated voice, sounding like a lawyer baldly stating a case.

Somehow Sheriff Oscar Brake of

Garrington had wandered in on the set-up: he had a nose for folks like Ben and Digo.

Ben had shot the lawman with the fancy little derringer which he had dropped afterwards, ruining it, letting it lay. It was that clue that had led Silvo and Temperly to the Double Curl where foreman Link had showed them the other half of the matching pair.

"Link always did have a fancy for one of them little weapons," said Rancher Lomass.

"How is Link?" Temperly asked. He had been so quick to tell the old man the worst, to lay it all out, to explain, that neither he or Silvo, or even Dooley who knew Link also, had asked about the young wounded foreman.

"Link's dead," said Lomass. "He took a turn for the worst." He looked at Silvo. "You knew him before, didn't you?"

"Yes," said Silvo.

"He was a wild one?"

"No wilder than me in them days, I

guess. Or Temp for that matter."

"No, an' that's a fact," said Temperly.

"He talked to my daughter Berenice before he died . . . "

"They wuz close, huh?" said Silvo.

"Not in the way you think maybe. Link wanted to marry Berenice. I was in two minds about it, wasn't sure at all. But Berenice turned him down anyway. She knew her half-brother Ben was a bad one. She treated Link like a real brother. She mourns for him . . . "

The old man's voice had become soft and sad again before it tailed off into silence. But that silence was not broken by either Silvo or Temperly as it was evident that Lomass had more to say, which he did.

"Link told Berenice that he'd been helping Ben and Digo an' their friends to milk the herd . . . "

"He allus wanted to be a cattleman, I think," put in Silvo. "And when he found that he couldn't marry the boss's daughter . . . "

There was no need to finish the

sentence, and Temperly took up the running again now. "So Link getting shot when we were drygulched was sort of an accident. He's been brought to death by his own friends."

"I don't guess that bunch were actually friends of his'n," said Silvo. "Except young Hideaway. But we were told that Digo set that up, weren't we? And he could've wanted Link outa the way, more pickin's for him an' Ben . . . "

"*What wickedness*," said Rancher Lomass. "I have been a hard man myself, I've had to be. And I've built . . . " He raised a large, gnarled hand and waved it slowly back and forth in front of him as if he was trying to brush away his own melancholy thoughts.

"But I've never . . . " Words momentarily failed him again. His leonine head drooped.

His next words were almost inaudible. "The herd . . . my boys will go . . . get it back . . . "

Berenice entered the big room. She inclined her head in a courteous motion to the two men but she did not speak right then. Her thick dark hair was immaculately groomed and she was heartbreakingly beautiful; and Cal Temperly knew that his friend Silvo couldn't take his eyes off her. And, in some strange way, there seemed to be a quality of rapport between them; had been, Temperly thought, from the very start.

Berenice's eyes were shadowed, dark rings under them. But she played the hostess without strain and her voice was kind. "Are you gentlemen going to stay, rest up?" It was as if she had known, sensed, what the news was, and had given it a grave acceptance.

Temperly said, "Thank you, Miss Berenice, but I have to be on my way. I have been away from home too long. I think my friend Dooley, when he comes back from the bunkhouse, will want to get back to his little horse-spread. I don't know about my friend Silvo. He'll have to speak for himself."

"I think I'll stick around for a while, Temp," said Silvo.

A complex, enigmatic man, with a wide streak of good in him which he tried to disguise; but that didn't always work.

The door was rapped and Dooley came in.

It was time for goodbyes to be exchanged.

As Temperly rode with Dooley, the oldster asked, "You coming into Garrington, Cal?"

"Just quickly, to say so-long to Jas and a few others, and to see old Silas and relinquish my acting-marshal's post. Then I'll be on my way."

On my way, he thought. Back to Tansy. Sweet Tansy with the big blue eyes and the corn-coloured hair . . .

FARGO: PANAMA GOLD
John Benteen

With foreign money behind him, Buckner was going to destroy the Panama Canal before it could be completed. Fargo's job was to stop Buckner.

FARGO: THE SHARPSHOOTERS
John Benteen

The Canfield clan, thirty strong were raising hell in Texas. Fargo was tough enough to hold his own against the whole clan.

PISTOL LAW
Paul Evan Lehman

Lance Jones came back to Mustang for just one thing — revenge! Revenge on the people who had him thrown in jail.

FARGO: MASSACRE RIVER
John Benteen

The ambushers up ahead had now blocked the road. Fargo's convoy was a jumble, a perfect target for the insurgents' weapons!

SUNDANCE: DEATH IN THE LAVA
John Benteen

The Modoc's captured the wagon train and its cargo of gold. But now the halfbreed they called Sundance was going after it . . .

HARSH RECKONING
Phil Ketchum

Five years of keeping himself alive in a brutal prison had made Brand tough and careless about who he gunned down . . .

SUNDANCE: SILENT ENEMY
John Benteen

A lone crazed Cheyenne was on a personal war path. They needed to pit one man against one crazed Indian. That man was Sundance.

LASSITER
Jack Slade

Lassiter wasn't the kind of man to listen to reason. Cross him once and he'll hold a grudge for years to come — if he let you live that long.

LAST STAGE TO GOMORRAH
Barry Cord

Jeff Carter, tough ex-riverboat gambler, now had himself a horse ranch that kept him free from gunfights and card games. Until Sturvesant of Wells Fargo showed up.

FIGHTING RAMROD
Charles N. Heckelmann

Most men would have cut their losses, but Frazer counted the bullets in his guns and said he'd soak the range in blood before he'd give up another inch of what was his.

LONE GUN
Eric Allen

Smoke Blackbird had been away too long. The Lequires had seized the Blackbird farm, forcing the Indians and settlers off, and no one seemed willing to fight! He had to fight alone.

THE THIRD RIDER
Barry Cord

Mel Rawlins wasn't going to let anything stand in his way. His father was murdered, his two brothers gone. Now Mel rode for vengeance.

McALLISTER ON THE COMANCHE CROSSING
Matt Chisholm

The Comanche, McAllister owes them a life — and the trail is soaked with the blood of the men who had tried to outrun them before.

QUICK-TRIGGER COUNTRY
Clem Colt

Turkey Red hooked up with Curly Bill Graham's outlaw crew. But wholesale murder was out of Turk's line, so when range war flared he bucked the whole border gang alone . . .

CAMPAIGNING
Jim Miller

Ambushed on the Santa Fe trail, Sean Callahan is saved by two Indian strangers. But there'll be more lead and arrows flying before the band join Kit Carson against the Comanches.

GUNSLINGER'S RANGE
Jackson Cole

Three escaped convicts are out for revenge. They won't rest until they put a bullet through the head of the dirty snake who locked them behind bars.

RUSTLER'S TRAIL
Lee Floren

Jim Carlin knew he would have to stand up and fight because he had staked his claim right in the middle of Big Ike Outland's best grass.

THE TRUTH ABOUT SNAKE RIDGE
Marshall Grover

The troubleshooters came to San Cristobal to help the needy. For Larry and Stretch the turmoil began with a brawl and then an ambush.

WOLF DOG RANGE
Lee Floren

Will Ardery would stop at nothing, unless something stopped him first — like a bullet from Pete Manly's gun.

DEVIL'S DINERO
Marshall Grover

Plagued by remorse, a rich old reprobate hired the Texas Troubleshooters to deliver a fortune in greenbacks to each of his victims.

GUNS OF FURY
Ernest Haycox

Dane Starr, alias Dan Smith, wanted to close the door on his past and hang up his guns, but people wouldn't let him.

BRETT RANDALL, GAMBLER
E. B. Mann

Larry Day had the choice of running away from the law or of assuming a dead man's place. No matter what he decided he was bound to end up dead.

THE GUNSHARP
William R. Cox

The Eggerleys weren't very smart. They trained their sights on Will Carney and Arizona's biggest blood bath began.

THE DEPUTY OF SAN RIANO
Lawrence A. Keating and
Al. P. Nelson

When a man fell dead from his horse, Ed Grant was spotted riding away from the scene. The deputy sheriff rode out after him and came up against everything from gunfire to dynamite.

HELL RIDERS
Steve Mensing

Wade Walker's kid brother, Duane, was locked up in the Silver City jail facing a rope at dawn. Wade was a ruthless outlaw, but he was smart, and he had vowed to have his brother out of jail before morning!

DESERT OF THE DAMNED
Nelson Nye

The law was after him for the murder of a marshal — a murder he didn't commit.. Breen was after him for revenge — and Breen wouldn't stop at anything ... blackmail, a frameup ... or murder.

DAY OF THE COMANCHEROS
Steven C. Lawrence

Their very name struck terror into men's hearts — the Comancheros, a savage army of cutthroats who swept across Texas, leaving behind a bloodstained trail of robbery and murder.

ARIZONA DRIFTERS
W. C. Tuttle

When drifting Dutton and Lonnie Steelman decide to become partners they find that they have a common enemy in the formidable Thurston brothers.

TOMBSTONE
Matt Braun

Wells Fargo paid Luke Starbuck to outgun the silver-thieving stagecoach gang at Tombstone. Before long Luke can see the only thing bearing fruit in this eldorado will be the gallows tree.

HIGH BORDER RIDERS
Lee Floren

Buckshot McKee and Tortilla Joe cut the trail of a border tough who was running Mexican beef into Texas. They stopped the smuggler in his tracks.